That Was Enough
An Immigrant's Tale of Hope and Resilience

by Peggy Glendenning

LITTLE CREEK PRESS
MINERAL POINT, WISCONSIN

Copyright © 2025 Peggy Glendenning

All rights reserved. No part of this publication may be reproduced, distributed, or transmitted in any form or by any means, including photocopying, recording, digital scanning, or other electronic or mechanical methods, without the prior written permission of the publisher, except in the case of brief quotations embodied in critical reviews and certain other noncommercial uses permitted by copyright law. For permission requests or other information, please send correspondence to the following address:

Little Creek Press
5341 Sunny Ridge Road
Mineral Point, WI 53565

ORDERING INFORMATION
Quantity sales. Special discounts are available on quantity purchases by corporations, associations, and others. For details, contact info@littlecreekpress.com

Orders by US trade bookstores and wholesalers.
Please contact Little Creek Press or Ingram for details.

Printed in the United States of America

Cataloging-in-Publication Data
Names: Peggy Glendenning, author
Title: That Was Enough: An Immigrant's Tale of Hope and Resilience
Description: Mineral Point, WI Little Creek Press, 2024
Identifiers: LCCN: 2025907502 | ISBN: 978-1-955656-99-3
Classification: FICTION / Family Life / General
FICTION / Sagas
FICTION / Small Town & Rural

Book design by Little Creek Press

This is a work of fiction. Some names, characters, places, and incidents are products of the author's imagination or are used fictitiously. Any resemblance to actual persons, living or dead, or actual events is purely coincidental. In certain cases, real names have been used with permission.

Dedicated to all those whose stories are never told,
whose voices are never heard, but who strive
to make a difference anyway.

That Was Enough

ILEARNED AT AN EARLY AGE HOW TO WALK IN A CEMETERY. My tiny, buckled shoes could barely keep up to the synchronized walk of my mother while trying valiantly to balance a spade and small bucket overflowing with flowers to be used as adornment near the gravestones. Seemed like a difficult task while making certain not to walk in a manner that my mother considered disrespectful amongst the dead. As if they minded my feathered steps across their final resting place. As if they would know that I accidentally shadowed across their burial site and then somehow curse me into damnation. Nonetheless, I proceeded as I was instructed.

Cemeteries carry their own presence, especially to a small child. They silently convey a sense of overwhelming peace and contentment. Even though we visit the dead there, everything else is very much alive and vibrant. The scent of cool, moist, black dirt; the pop of purple in the grass from the overrun creeping Charlie; and the wind that provides perpetual breezes as if a soul is whispering its last loving message to a somber visitor. For me, tagging along with my almost silent mother, I experienced a plethora of senses. The tantalizing sounds of spring, the return of lovely birds singing gloriously, and the excitement in anticipation of another season spent outdoors. Mother rarely spoke while we knelt in the damp soil and decorated one stone at a time belonging to those I had never met. She would lovingly disrupt a small area of dirt and carefully plant the blooming beauty. Her hands moved in such mesmerizing motion, as if conducting a symphony before angels. Her rhythmic motions were soothing and tender to the eye. I watched in wonder at these soft, caring moments, not understanding a thing about it. I also couldn't understand why these beautiful cross-shaped headstones that Mother took such care of were located near the back of the cemetery, a noticeable distance from the other resting souls. Even at a tender age, I was curious about their placement. I imagined that if it rained, this area would collect all the rainwater from the entire cemetery—a thought I quickly purged from my mind. The whole process of pulling weeds, adornment, and silence seemed like a waste of good play time, but those timeworn stones meant something to my mother, and that was enough.

The stones were made of white Carrara marble, and there were three of them. Their stark white color was unique against the many shades of early spring greens and the darker gray of most other stones. They stood steadfast against time, holding their humble life story peacefully beneath the earth's surface. With each passing year, the roots of grass lay down another intricate blanket of forgetfulness. The stones weren't majestic or grand, but at a certain time of day, they caught the sunlight perfectly to emit a heavenly beacon of reflected light, somehow projecting a feeling of perpetual hope to my young heart and mind.

Once back in our car, where apparently it was now okay to make a sound and have an actual conversation, Mother would tell me stories about the three people who now rest eternally beneath those headstones. Every year she shared a different story of a hardship or jovial moment, and every year I just nodded as I stared out the window obliviously, wondering what we would be having for dinner or what game I might play when we arrived home. Mother was speaking to me but wasn't really talking to me, just aloud to herself, I suppose, bringing back a happy time in her memory closet. A time when someone she knew stood brave, strong, and proud. I didn't know then where this place she called Italy was. I could not identify with the struggles Mother spoke of, and I never met those she reverently discussed. But somehow, I knew that had it not been for the bravery and sacrifice of these people, my life would've been very different.

One

Italy 1904. Concetta was barely twenty-four when her mother called her into the summer kitchen from the garden. It was a hot, mid-summer afternoon, and the Calabrian countryside was alive with beauty and soul. Concetta and her son, 3 yr old Samuel, were delightfully enjoying all aspects of the bountiful vegetable garden. She tried to keep up with the giggles and toddling of her young son as he enjoyed running up and down the many long rows of lush edibles. Row after row of beautiful fruits and vegetables were bursting from the sandy soil that created a cloud of fine dust behind the footsteps of Samuel as he rounded each corner. Concetta especially loved the succulent scents floating about the garden air as it exhaled. Each row emitted a unique and glorious aroma that awakened even the weakest of senses. Her olfactory system gave her a choice of favorites. She was particularly fond of the scent of basil, followed closely by the sturdy, fuzzy tomato plant aroma, which always beckoned her to sample its sweet, juicy flavor. More than one tomato had disappeared during the walk from the garden to the kitchen due to Concetta's powerlessness over the juicy delight.

Summers in southern Italy could be scorching, and this summer was no different. Many a neighbor had complained to Concetta about the difficulties of spending time in the searing summer heat and the hard, laborious work. Still, Concetta adored being out, despite the heat. She met each day with both eyes wide open, thankful for the gift of another day and enjoying every moment she was given. The hot sun was like a gift to Concetta, providing her with warmth and contentment. She was mindful and savored all the surrounding gifts of nature that blessed her day. She particularly loved the way the top of the olive trees seemed to reach out and sway, calling forth the sun's rays. As if choreographed by God, it was like an intricate ballet between the sun and the tree spirit.

Concetta's quaint home and property also emitted an undeniable, inviting glow. The warm, dry breeze that billowed the bedding she hung on the clothesline in the early mornings was hypnotic and intoxicating as the air movement and cotton engaged in dance. The purple bougainvillea plants surrounding Concetta's little stone cottage were as welcoming to Concetta as they were to many a visitor. The countryside view from the narrow path up to the garden was nothing short of a spiritual journey. The hills reflected stunning color, occasionally pierced by a tall cypress tree or flowering shrub. Mother and son typically spent hours every day enjoying the paradise they were fortunate to call home. On this day, it would be a shout coming from the summer kitchen inviting them in for some freshly squeezed lemonade, perfected by the hand of Concetta's mother, Maria. This invitation was enticing enough to call an end to their morning in the sun. Concetta retrieved the basket of vegetable bounty and caught up to Samuel as they skipped toward the summer kitchen.

Concetta and Samuel came through the doorway hand in hand. His little tanned face was brushed with dusty limestone left behind by the kiss of the wind. Maria reached down and swooped Samuel up. She so enjoyed having her daughter and grandson back home in the little stone cottage, despite the tragedy that preceded their homecoming. Concetta's husband, Samuel's father, had perished in the last big earthquake in the fall of last year during olive picking.

Each family in the village helped the other during the olive harvest. Concetta's husband, the handsome Antonio, was in the groves with many other men picking the olives. The ground began to shake, alerting the group to danger. Antonio and the other men rushed to their dwellings to protect their families. Antonio reached the doorway as his wife and child curled up under the table together. They both watched Antonio hurrying to join them. Moments before reaching the safety of the table, a large stone fell, striking his head. He was knocked to the ground, briefly unconscious and dazed.

Somehow, Antonio scrambled beneath the table and rode out the rest of the earth's tremble with his family. When the shaking stopped, Concetta was able to address Antonio's wound. It appeared to be just a slight wound, not much bleeding at all. Antonio reassured Concetta he was fine as he waited patiently beneath the table to ensure the quake was over. That night when Antonio went to sleep, his eyes closed for the last time. Concetta stood vigil for three days by Antonio's side praying he would wake. However, he succumbed to his injury. Such tragedy and sadness for a young family to endure. Concetta's parents now took over the responsibilities of Antonio's land, and Concetta moved home to grieve their tragic loss and move ahead living without her dear Antonio.

Concetta grieved for the loss of her husband but also needed to move forward for her growing son. Tragedy was everywhere in Europe, and it had no boundaries. Many Italian lives were plagued with tragedy in one form or another. This was not to say they were complacent about tragedy, but just experienced in managing it. Concetta didn't know any family that hadn't suffered a loss or tragedy of their own. Loss and hardship were a normal way of living, which no doubt gave her the gratitude for each day she was granted. Now it was about surviving and learning to accept the things one could not change and continue with life. Adaptation was a valuable life skill all too often learned at an early age by tragedy.

The tartness of the lemon in the fresh lemonade made Samuel grimace, causing laughter between the two women seated around the rectangular table adorned with a faded linen cloth. Oh, how Concetta loved that faded cloth. It represented so many memories and times of complete comfort and bliss. It was as if the tablecloth told a lifelong story with its mixture of unexposed color unspoiled by protection from hours in the elements and other more exposed areas that grew pale in color due to heat, sun, and excessive washings. Concetta allowed herself to relax and breathe in the moment. The blazing sun was high in the sky as the temperatures soared. She wiped moisture from her bronze brow with a soft handkerchief given to her by her father, which prompted her to inquire, "Is Father joining us?" Concetta questioned her mother.

"Yes, he will be coming shortly. You know him. He's always checking the olives. Day in day out, like they are his babies!" Maria chuckled as she threw both hands in the air.

A more serious tone quickly replaced Maria's joking manner of speech.

"Concetta, word has come from America," she began. "Remember Francesco Nardi? Vito's son from across the valley?"

"The one who went to America?" Concetta asked.

"Yes, you have a good memory," Maria praised. "It seems that tragedy has befallen him, and his wife has died."

Concetta felt sad and empathetic for poor Francesco. She remembered his kind words and actions when she was a little girl. Although he was eight years her senior, he'd often spoken a kind word to her in passing. Now he had suffered the same devastating loss of a spouse that she had endured. How would he manage without the support of family?

"Poor man," Concetta sympathized. "He must feel so alone in America." Concetta had the strength of her mother and father to hold her together when Antonio died. She had the love and needs of Antonio's child, Samuel, to keep her busy and focused and the perseverance of being a strong young woman to challenge herself to keep moving forward. What did Francesco have?

"An interesting observation you've made, Concetta," Maria stated as her husband pulled open the screen door to join them.

Giovanni entered the summer kitchen, stretching out both arms toward little Samuel, inviting him into the haven of Nonno's arms. Samuel jumped forward, feet barely touching the floor, until he reached the spot both were anticipating, followed by a quick launch into the air and a warm hug landing. Both women beamed at the sight of grandfather and grandson entwined in such a moment. Could there be a more perfect expression of love between those two? Giovanni was small in stature but large in life. He sported a handlebar mustache that had long ago turned gray. His perfectly tanned olive skin was a telltale sign of his many hours spent in the warm Calabrian sun. He always wore white shirts, much to Maria's dismay. He would joke with Maria that the white shirt made him easier for her to spot at a distance, so she would recognize her true love even from afar. As he sat down to pour and enjoy a refreshing glass of lemonade, he lowered Samuel to the ground. The breeze picked up and tossed Giovanni's hair about. He spoke as he swept the hair away from his leathery-colored, sweaty forehead.

"Now, Concetta, your mother tells me we have news to share from America,"

Giovanni cautiously stated as he gestured to Maria to finally reveal more of this mysterious information that apparently required a family discussion.

"We are here, all together," Maria began as she reached out and took Concetta and Giovanni by the hand.

"Francesco has written to us, Concetta, asking our permission to send you to America to be his wife." Maria's eyes lowered in such a way that it could not be determined if she was thankful or terrified. Giovanni eyed Concetta, and she returned his stare as if not understanding what had just happened. The room fell completely silent, except for the distant ping of a metal pie tin in the garden, as it moved rhythmically with the wind striking against the wooden post, not to be outdone by the slapping of Samuel's hands on the small piece of bread dough his grandmother had given him to play with. It was as if, for a slight moment, all time had ceased, and the breeze was listening for an answer.

"This is the chance of a lifetime, my darling. A chance for Samuel and you to find a better life. One with happiness and contentment in America! A dream comes true! You will have a man to take care of the two of you and a grand life in America," Giovanni said convincingly as he began eating his sandwich.

Concetta wasn't certain if he was attempting to convince her or himself. Perhaps a bit of both. *What could possibly be better than the beautiful life we have here in Italy?* she thought.

"But the decision is yours to make, my dear. Just keep in mind that your mother and I only want the best for you and our darling Samuel. We will not live forever," concluded Giovanni with pooling eyes.

"This is something to consider, my dears. We will talk more about it tomorrow. Now for a little more of that refreshing lemonade, my dear sainted wife!" Giovanni said as he seemed to quickly dismiss the heartbreaking thought of potential separation from his daughter and grandson.

The three sat in the summer kitchen talking and laughing together over the bright yellow lemonade as Samuel skipped around the perimeter, singing sweet Italian songs. Soon the sun was moving lower in the western sky, and it was time to begin supper. The temperature was more forgiving with the setting of the sun, and it made indoor chores a bit more tolerable. On this night, however, the only chore achieved was constructing a delicious meal.

Concetta's time was consumed with thoughts and dreams of magical living in America. She could not resist the excitement she felt at the prospect of traveling to America. She had been told so many enchanting stories of excitement and intrigue regarding America. Such an endeavor would take her far from home and her family, but surely, with all the wealth available in America, she could return to her homeland at will to visit her beloved parents. As is the way of youth, Concetta gave little thought to the consequences of the journey and what the prospect of leaving their homeland truly meant. Young Italians were leaving the country by the thousands in search of their fortunes and a better life. It was, after all, a new century, and the opportunities available were not only astounding but enticing! The prospect allowed Concetta to entertain excitement again within her heart. Was there a beat that still existed within her heart that could allow her to make such a journey toward a new life and husband? Was she truly ready to move on without Antonio? Move forward with a man she barely knew?

Concetta's mind was distant with thought as she ate the fresh tuna on focaccia bread she had prepared for supper. Even the juice from the fresh sliced tomato that dripped on Concetta's hand was wiped away on her apron instead of savored on her tongue as was typically her custom. There was so much to think about, so much to consider. Did she really remember what kind of man Francesco was? Did she ever really know what kind of man he was? Had America changed him? She had always liked Francesco, and he would make a good father for Samuel. She continued to ponder as she lay the child down for the night, pausing to stroke his dark, soft hair. He looked so much like his father, with his perfectly tanned skin and dark hair. Moreover, he had inherited Antonio's joyful spirit and charm. Samuel was content with all things, spreading joy to each day, and the perfect mix of angelic beauty and devilish grin. How could she possibly consider anything but acceptance for this generous opportunity? Imagine what Samuel could experience in America and what opportunities he would have there. She felt a sense of responsibility to Samuel to facilitate this incredible opportunity. At least, that's what she told herself.

Concetta then retreated to the summer kitchen, her favorite indoor place to reflect. She was not surprised to find her father there as well. Giovanni and Concetta were cut from the same cloth. Both were strong, adventurous, and fiercely loving. As they sat together with only the table between them, both were aware there was no real decision to be made, for the chance to go to America was like a golden key to the giant door of an enchanting castle—an opportunity spared for only those lucky enough to receive it. It was merely facing the reality and what that would mean to the close-knit family.

"Please, my dear, share your thoughts," offered Giovanni as he patted the chair next to him in a motion for her to sit.

As Concetta slipped into the wooden chair next to her father, she heard the familiar, endearing sound of the nighthawk screeching outside in the warm Mediterranean night air.

"What shall we discuss, my little one?" Giovanni questioned lovingly.

"Oh, Papa, to go to America and live a dream is more than I could've ever hoped for. When Antonio died, I thought the door to my future happiness had closed," explained Concetta.

"Yes, my dear. I would agree," he consented. Despite his carefully concealed sadness, Giovanni knew the right choice was for Concetta to leave for America. Now how to convince his heavy heart of this.

"Tomorrow we shall begin the process of passage for you and Samuel to go to America. My darling daughter, I love you with all my heart, and I'll always want what is best for you and my Samuel. I shall dream for you a magnificent garden in America," Giovanni stated with momentum in his voice.

It was all he could do to get the words out. No matter how secure a future would be for his darling loved ones in America, he wanted them to stay here … to live out their days together with Maria and him, to run each day together in the warm Calabrian sun, and to watch little Samuel grow.

Concetta and Giovanni allowed the hours to pass by as they discussed many topics, from the old way things were accomplished in the olive groves to the method of care given to the olive groves today. The content of their conversation wasn't as important as the act. Both enjoyed each other's company immensely, but only Giovanni realized how much they would miss these late-night conversations. This tender exchange between a daughter and her father would become a priceless memory destined to be revisited repeatedly by each of them in the years ahead.

A short night gave way to another brilliant sunrise over the Calabrian countryside. The rolling hills, in all their glory, were awakening with the first light of day. The sheer curtains of the small room where Concetta and Samuel slept were still waving in slow motion but vibrant with light. Samuel stirred in his bed as Concetta quietly slipped on her stockings and shoes.

Giovanni was already up and preparing to head into Lamezia. There he would secure passage and obtain the proper documentation for his daughter and grandson to journey to America. He hugged his daughter tightly as the neighbor Matteo rode up the walk in his horse-drawn wagon. She waved and watched her father disappear over the blooming hillside. *Today is the beginning of a new and different life for Samuel and me*, Concetta thought.

Two

The next few weeks were merely a blur of daily chores and travel preparation for Concetta. She kept busy thinking of America and its shining streets of gold she had heard so much about. Then, one day, it was THE day that Concetta and Samuel would begin their great journey across the Atlantic Sea to America.

Departure day proved to be a bit more difficult than Concetta had anticipated. She awoke to the same golden sun and the only horizon she'd ever known and was just beginning to absorb the reality of its finality. This would be the last morning she would wake to the sights and sounds of Calabria. At least until she could save enough money to return, she bravely thought to douse her concerns. As the family assembled in the summer kitchen to distribute their goodbyes, Concetta was mindful of the strength of her father's heart beating to hold back his tears as he pulled his greatest treasure close to him in what would prove to be an unknowing final embrace. His calloused hands and big soft heart seemed clumsy and held no purpose for him now. Maria was virtually a silent pillar of strength whose careworn face now contorted into a well-controlled pain, not unlike the application of an ancient torture tactic that slowly tears one in two. It was a moment of sheer pain, as any parent can imagine when bidding farewell to a child. A grown child who, saddened by the circumstance but excited at the prospect of new beginnings, needed to find the strength to say goodbye.

One last kiss goodbye was afforded as the footfalls of Matteo, the neighbor, approached their humble home. He would take Concetta and Samuel to the docks for their journey, as he had much experience in taking many a young, adventurous Italian to the ships. Matteo was a good man, a good neighbor, and the only one with a horse and buggy. Giovanni and Maria stood outside their stone cottage in Calabria waving goodbye to their beautiful daughter and young grandson, painfully aware they would probably never see them again. They would never delight in their grandson's milestones and never watch him become a man. Their beautiful daughter would grow old beyond their sight. Life's changes and trepidations would not be shared between the loving family now separated by change, progress, and a vast ocean.

They wept openly and without control now, attempting to console each other in an inconsolable situation. Concetta watched and waved to her parents until distance melted away their shadowy figures. "It will be fine; I will come back to see them as soon as I can," Concetta said to herself, hoping to conceal the feeling of finality within her heart. Then, the wagon rounded a bend, and just like that, the cottage was gone, her parents were gone, and the beautiful life that began in Calabria was over, just but a memory of the heart now. Concetta held tight to Samuel, promising him a bright future filled with a multitude of opportunities. It was the first day of their new life, and they would face it with anticipation and gratitude.

The ship was enormous as it stood floating in the port. For the first time, Concetta began to feel uneasy. This would be the vessel that carried them across the seemingly endless ocean. Even tucked safely in the harbor, it looked cold, unfeeling, and dangerously dark—a massive wooden vessel that cast an ugly shadow across the pier crawling with activity. Concetta had never been to the port before. *Where on earth are all these people going?* she thought. She had, however, heard tragic stories and tales from the sea. A feeling of hypnotic reality had struck Concetta. Had it not been for Matteo lightly touching her shoulder, she may have never left the wagon that day. She climbed down cautiously so as not to wake Samuel, who had fallen asleep with the rocking motion of the wagon. Matteo carried Concetta's small bag, which held every item that represented Concetta and Samuel's life up until this moment, as he escorted her to the ship. *One small bag, such a tiny amount of proof of a life well lived*, thought Concetta. A tiny testament to the love and security they had turned and easily, or perhaps not so easily, walked away from. Tiny physical proof, but her heart was filled with memories, love for her parents, and that was enough. For now, it would have to be.

Matteo instructed Concetta to watch her belongings and speak to no one aboard the vessel. Someone would be waiting for her in America when she was allowed entry. Concetta hugged and thanked Matteo for the ride and requested he look after her parents while she was away. Matteo graciously agreed, as he had always enjoyed the company of Giovanni and Maria. He handed Concetta her small bag, and she wobbled up the plank into the ship carrying Samuel.

On board she was met by a small man in a black suit. He asked for her papers, and she obliged. She was instructed to head to the left and down the dark, steep steps to a lower compartment where she could find an area to call her own for the next several days. Even in the dimly lit compartment, Concetta could see the confines and restrictions of her travel accommodations. *At least there is a bed*, thought Concetta, using her positive attitude. She was brave and resilient. After all, this was temporary. She had endured many bigger challenges with lesser rewards. Concetta gingerly sat on the edge of the thin makeshift mattress and held Samuel to her chest. His long eyelashes were so mesmerizing when he slept, like long wisps of a gentle broom that could sweep you off your feet in an instant. One day, she would tell him of their journey together across the sea. One day, they would smile and laugh about this day. One day, she would express to him how her love for him was the driving force that allowed her to put one foot in front of the other. She began to focus on dreams of what could lie ahead in America as she gently kissed Samuel's forehead.

Her thoughts of pleasantry were disrupted by the creaks and snaps of the ship beginning to move. Concetta worked her way to a porthole window, as did many of the other passengers. The boardwalk appeared to be moving, along with hundreds of people, no doubt containing Matteo, waving toward the ship. It took a moment for Concetta to realize it was the ship that was moving, for it was slow and steady.

"So far, so good," she whispered to Samuel, stroking his sleepy head. "We can do this, my darling."

Concetta watched the unknown faces of those left standing on the pier until they became just ink blots on the horizon. Melting away, along with her past, like an ice cube on a hot afternoon.

Concetta was strong and brave as the ship set sail that day, ready to face whatever lay ahead to secure her son's future and her own. She had no idea how strong she was or how strong she would become. However, several days in steerage took its toll on Concetta. Samuel seemed to be adjusting well, always the content child, able to be entertained by the smallest detail. Concetta made finger puppets from some rags she located under their meager bunk area. They played on the deck at times and sang songs and rhymes. They watched birds soaring overhead, imagining where they were from and where they were going.

The deck was such a vibrant, bustling place. So many people making this faith-filled journey! So much chaos, excitement, and constant noise. Some travelers seemed genuinely elated to be going to America, but for most in steerage, the reality of missing home was beginning to sting the heart. The never-ending motion of the ship, the constant whimpers from someone in pain, whether it be physical or mental anguish, were both exhausting and heartbreaking to listen to. Each night in the sleeping quarters, one young girl, who appeared to be about fourteen years old, would call out in the night for her mother. They were heartbreaking cries that echoed deep within each passenger. Everyone aboard had their story, which they seemed to guard as tightly as their last priceless heirloom. Concetta felt many a tear sliding down her cheek as she thought of her own mother's love and the little stone cottage in the beautiful Calabrian countryside. What she wouldn't have given at that moment to be transported home, forget the whole journey, and live out her life in the safety of that glorious place.

Why was I so eager to leave? Is Mama crying for me? Why didn't I look back just one more time? she thought.

She looked down at Samuel's sleeping face. So angelic, so innocent and content just to be loved. Would he ever remember the loving grandparents they left behind? Concetta leaned back against a large beam that somehow found itself against the bottom of their makeshift bed. Had she done the right thing? Made the right choice? She closed her eyes and remembered the smell of her mother baking bread. She could imagine the scent of the lard and flour as she recalled her mother's hands kneading the dough. The even rhythm of her palms meeting with the dough as a tiny cloud of flour tried to keep up with the motions. The smooth, charming thoughts of Concetta's memory relaxed her enough to allow her mind to drift into a sleep-like state. Concetta could see the loaf sliding out of the oven on the long-handled wooden peel. She could hear the wind sweeping through the leaves just behind the giant outdoor oven as if she were standing there. She visualized the ancient wooden table under her favorite shade tree where the fresh bread was sometimes placed to cool. The same wooden table that occasionally hosted a hungry appetite for that warm, fresh bread along with a glass of her uncle's red wine shared with her husband. Even now, in dreams, she could taste the sweetness of the wine, hear the laughter of Antonio while they enjoyed the delicious bread and togetherness. With eyes closed, she was blissfully back home in Calabria, even if it was just in the dream part of her heart.

A few moments of peaceful dream were short-lived as the ship lurched to one side, apparently hit by a strong wave. Moments later, the ship was being tossed about violently. The noise of the wooden hull creaking with every peak and dip of the sail was terrifying. Those who had been resting or dreaming of a new world were suddenly brought into the moment. Samuel awoke and began to cry. Concetta tried her best to calm him, but her ebony eyes were also ablaze with fear. She strained to look out at the sea from a tiny port window across from another bunk. Dark, turbulent waves were all she could see. Peaks and valleys tossed together so violently they turned parts of the dark water white. Most of the children were now sobbing, and many parents were sobbing too. As Concetta scanned the eyes of the men in the room for a reaction to this sudden change, she found only fear looking back at her. Everyone aboard knew that a storm at sea was nothing to flirt with for many a soul had met their fate to an angry sea.

As Concetta reached into the pocket of her faded cotton sweater, her fingertips recalled the smooth familiarity of her rosary. She clutched the cross and began to remove it from her pocket, each bead emerging from the pocket like a rope of life vests being strung into the ocean. As Samuel sat fearfully quiet on her lap, she began to pray. Prayer had always been her source of comfort, her source of great strength, a guide for her heart to follow in uncertain times and situations. Concetta could now hear the mutterings of many passengers in a low hum of prayer despite the loud sounds coming from outside.

The hum was abruptly stopped by the slamming sound of the large deck door a crew member latched closed. Seeing this man throwing the door closed without a word of caution or indication why was a terrifying sight. A few aboard knew why and began instructing others to stow away any loose items, cling tightly to their children, and find a safe area to ride out the storm. It was now that the darkness would come. The blackened, lonely darkness that to Concetta was, quite possibly, the face of death. Was this to be their destiny? Concetta mustered up all her courage and faith. She promised God that if he granted Samuel and her life in a new land, she would accept His will for the rest of her days.

After more than an hour of being tossed by the sea, the darkness gave way to the sounds of wailing children, injured passengers who were thrown about, and the smell of vomit and spilled chamber pots. Although conditions were barely tolerable, Concetta continued to pray through her fear. Her faith was incredibly strong, and she had accepted that the storm was God's will and would be His will if they survived. The ship stopped rocking as quickly as it had begun. Deafening sounds of terror and destruction were now calmed by the moans and exhausted sighs of the passengers. Survival had endured as none were lost that day. For those still able to gather thoughts, it was a time of silent gratitude to God, who had spared them from what they anticipated to be a watery grave, at least for now. The same crew member who had thrown the large deck door shut hours earlier opened it again. The rectangular opening emitted a ray of early morning light that signaled the dawn of another day. A night of terror that surrendered itself to a glorious sunrise. Concetta noticed several passengers had abrasions and scrapes from being tossed about during the storm. She offered thanks that she and Samuel were spared any injury.

Four days ago, Samuel and Concetta had been sitting in the little stone cottage, safe, dry, healthy, happy, and satisfied to be alive. What was she thinking embarking on this terrible journey alone with a small child? Was it a bit of self-pity or perhaps the lack of sleep that filled her eyes with tears as she scanned the room around her? Through her pooled eyes she could see the faces of so many just like her who were searching and hoping for a better life in America. Tired, weary faces, young, hopeful faces, and old accepting faces. Each face held on to an unspoken story that was as unique and inspiring as it was similar and real. Their story of life, according to each of them. *There are so many*, Concetta thought, yet she felt so alone. Hundreds of travelers, she estimated, all with little more than a dream of America to sustain them. Row after row of bunks, each occupied by a similar story of wishes. Concetta wondered how tattered she must look to the unknowing fellow traveler. Did they know the fear and homesickness that lingered in her heart? Was her fear visible to the outside world? Were they just as afraid and homesick as she? What awaited them all upon arrival? How would she communicate? What would she do if Francesco wasn't there for her?

Concetta and Samuel shared a bunk on the bottom side of the rows. The woman occupying the bunk beside them spoke an unfamiliar language while praying. It sounded like a type of Ukrainian to Concetta, but she couldn't be certain. The two women could not communicate with words, but the Ukrainian woman had kind, pale eyes that conveyed a sense of calm and reassurance for Concetta. The fair-eyed woman was much older than Concetta, rarely got out of bed, and seemed very weak. Her clothes were tattered, and she expelled a strong odor of lingering filth. Her timeworn hands seemed stiff and untouched by cleansing. Despite her condition, she reached out with a thankful hand to accept the piece of bread Concetta handed her. Concetta's father had instructed her to only eat bread and water aboard the vessel.

"This would help with the seasickness," he promised. Concetta wasn't sure this was true, but she followed her father's instructions. She did not have a great abundance of bread for her and Samuel but knew she needed to share with the woman as Concetta had not seen her journey to far from the bed the entire voyage.

"The Lord would provide," Concetta murmured to herself as she stretched out her hand holding the bread. The woman gave a gentle nod of gratitude as she stretched out her leathery hand and accepted it. Later that evening Concetta noticed most of the bread was left uneaten.

"Please," Concetta said to the Ukrainian woman as she gestured toward the uneaten bread. The woman just gave a reluctant nod and closed her eyes. Concetta was perplexed, but she continued to offer encouragement to the stricken woman any way she could. What would possess this lonely soul to journey so far in such a frail state?

After what seemed like many months, when in truth was just eleven days, the excitement of land spotted ahead spread through the ship like so many infectious diseases had. This time, the news was glorious and terrifying all at once. Just beyond the deck door was America! The gateway to hope, the promise of a better life, and the most frightful thoughts one could summon. Concetta could now hear the shouting of men on the dock. What a combination of terror and excitement came over her! They had made it! She had conquered the first milestone in beginning a new life. Tears of utter exhaustion and gratefulness ran uncontrollably down the cheeks of many. The passengers patiently waited several hours in the dark, damp ship for the final arrival on solid land. The smell of the wet wood, kerosene, and filth had long since faded as the overpowering sensation it had once been. For all aboard, however, these smells would remain woven into the fabric of their memory, to be carried as a companion for the rest of their days.

Concetta and Samuel anxiously awaited freedom from the sea, but unloading the ship would take time. All at once, the great door opened, and a plank was guided to the opening. It took a few moments for Concetta's eyes to adjust to the brightness of the light filtering in spilling onto the filthy wooden floor. Once she could focus on her surroundings, her eyes quickly darted to the Ukrainian woman. The woman had risen by her own power and was now fixated on the opening with what appeared to be a new found hope. Concetta uttered the word "please," as she gestured with an outstretched palm inviting the woman to exit ahead of her and Samuel. The women wobbly at first began to trod toward the opening. She paused to pat Samuel on the head and softly touched Concetta's cheek with an understanding, grateful gesture. They all exchanged a smile, for this was an understanding that bared no language barrier. Concetta gathered their meager belongings and scooped up Samuel, leaving behind the horror of the ship. She stepped as if she were a beautiful white dove finally breaking free from her snare. Concetta took a first step onto the plank that connected the ship to the pier. She was cautious and moved slowly following directly behind the frail woman. *Where does her strength come from?* Concetta thought as one by one they reached the shredded wooden edge of the plank. For one fraction of a moment, time completely stopped again, and Concetta valiantly stepped down from the plank that linked her to a new enchanting world. The past would be left behind in the crumbs and tears that fell onto the ship's floor. That brave, uncertain step would alter the course of a family's history—of thousands of families' histories.

The chaos and confusion on the pier were unlike anything Concetta had ever seen. This was nothing like the piers she was familiar with. However, she had very little knowledge of European piers in general. Finally, the sunlight warmed their faces, and Concetta found herself standing hand in hand on the pier with Samuel. In the near distance stood an incredible statue that held captive the attention of each disembarking passenger. It was her, THE statue that Concetta had been told about. The Statue of Liberty. In her hand, she held an immense flame to illuminate each hopeful immigrant's soul on the path of the promise of a bright tomorrow. No earthly words could describe the feeling inside an immigrant's heart as they lay their tired eyes upon her. Many were openly weeping or wailing their undying gratitude before this grand lady. In all the excitement and awe, Concetta lost sight of the Ukrainian woman. She hoped there was someone to vouch for her and that she would find happiness in this new land. Concetta felt a sense of sadness that she had lost sight of this woman whom she never really knew, but shared an incredible experience with. *I'll keep her in my prayers,* thought Concetta. The majesty of the statue was soon overtaken by the realization that the group of new arrivals was being funneled onto another floating vessel. Concetta thought it was some kind of American ferry. She couldn't help but observe that only second- and third-class passengers had boarded this ferry. Another overwhelming sense of terror enveloped her. *What if we are not allowed to enter? Where are they taking us? What if we are forced to return to Italy after completing such a long, exhausting journey? Could they really turn us away with the eyes of that beautiful statue gazing down upon us, reflecting such great hope and acceptance for each of us? Could we possibly be turned away in front of her?* This great statue's eyes looked so soft and welcoming, as if to say, "Come into my land, for your journey was a difficult one. Be at peace within my border." Another passenger called her the Statue of Liberty, too. Her name was not important to Concetta. The statue was beautiful, encouraging, and somehow inspiring. Wasn't that enough?

There was no room to sit on the ferry. Samuel played on the wooden planked deck floor for a short time. Alas, this short playtime quickly passed as the floor soon became wet and soiled with seawater and human waste. Passengers stood shoulder to shoulder for what seemed like an eternity. No explanation was presented for this seclusion and delay. The last small piece of bread in Concetta's pocket could've helped to satisfy Samuel's whimpers of hunger, but Concetta was fearful of presenting any food where it could be seen. Other passengers were starving as well and surely would've injured Concetta or Samuel to acquire something to eat, however small. They had all become desperate for basic human needs. It was survival and fear they battled now.

The sun was warm but thankfully not as piercing as the Calabrian sun. Water would've been a welcome sight, and each yearned for a drink. Using the sun's position, Concetta estimated they had been on the ferry for approximately five hours.

Maybe they are hoping we will all perish on this ferry, and we'll be dumped into the sea, she thought.

It was little Samuel who, as always, kept her moving forward and gave her encouragement and faith. Concetta busied herself reaffirming and instilling faith in Samuel that they would eat and drink soon. Looking ahead to an uncertain future that was not yet written, Concetta promised her reflection in Samuel's eyes that she would become the author of their future, at least until the quill could be passed to Samuel.

Suddenly, people began to move. At long last, the new arrivals were permitted to set foot on Ellis Island. The curators at this tiny island herded the large crowd of immigrants into the main hall of a huge building. Although she felt like one sheep in a large herd, she followed them. They were funneled into individual lines where they stood silently waiting their turn to speak to a large man wearing a hat seated at a table with another smaller man. She couldn't help but wonder why a man would wear a hat indoors. Removing one's hat was an insistence upon entering a dwelling in her experience. She laughed to herself. *How entertaining,* she thought, *as I stand here with my young son in this great hall, on American soil for the first time, not knowing what the next minute holds for us, and all I can think of is this man's hat.*

Concetta watched the two men as she waited in line for whatever it was that they were waiting for. She had no idea what would happen next. Her anxiety began to grow as she thought about what awaited her beyond the walls of this building. Would she recognize Francesco? What if he'd changed his mind and wasn't even there? What if she didn't like America? What if

Francesco didn't approve of her or Samuel? How would her parents survive without her and Samuel? So many questions in her mind. She became aloft with the hypnotic swaying of the moving line.

Suddenly, she heard a deep voice say, "Senora?" It was the dark-haired, large man with the hat. He couldn't help but notice Concetta's coal-black hair, her dark almond-shaped eyes, and her lovely olive-colored skin. The man stopped to pause and take in all her beauty.

"What is your name, senora?" asked the man. He waited for her answer while looking Concetta up and down. Although she did not know what the man said, she felt a shiver up her spine from his unwelcome stare. He asked again, "What is your name, senora?"

The larger man with the hat turned to the smaller man and said something Concetta also did not understand. Both men broke out in laughter, and one nudged the other with his elbow.

"Look, miss, we need to write a name down in this book, see?" the smaller man said a bit louder, motioning with his pen.

Concetta's heart began to race. She couldn't understand a word they were saying. Why didn't she prepare better? Why did she think they would speak her language? *What am I going to do?* she thought. Then she felt a warm hand on her shoulder. A fair-haired woman with a German accent said to Concetta, "Come ti chiami?" She pointed at the two men seated at the table.

"Ah, si," Concetta answered. How could she not have figured out they were asking for a name? *Silly girl, take your time and think*, she thought to herself. She promptly told the men her name and the name of her son. Concetta watched as the man used an ink pen to scribble each of their names into a large ledger book. When he finished writing the names, he moved his large right hand and waved it above the book in a motion for her to move on. A simple action, really, but to Concetta it was as if he was sweeping her entire past off the table. To say, it no longer is of value to you, and you must forget all. How easy he made it look to dismiss someone. Did he know or understand what it took for each of these souls standing in this line just to get to this point? Was he aware of the sacrifices? Was he concerned about these wonderfully talented and loving people who risked everything they'd ever known and now cannot even understand the language he is speaking? Did he even care? Where would each traveler locate kindness, compassion, and a

22 THAT WAS ENOUGH

simple place to rest, something they all craved at this point?

As Concetta followed the path of streaming new arrivals, she noticed many displayed chalk markings on their jackets or dresses. Another unknown situation, she decided. Concetta's hopes wavered slightly as she and Samuel neared yet another line. A young boy was scanning the crowd and approached Concetta. He took his chalk and marked the collar of her dress, then smiled at her and moved on. At the front of this line, a man who must've been a physician was looking in mouths and on scalps of each immigrant. Some people were marked yet again, and some were not. Each was directed to the right or left. When Concetta and Samuel reached the doctor, he quickly examined each of them. He spoke to her in limited Italian, but his tone was kind.

"Are you traveling alone? Have you been ill? Is there a bond posted for you and your child?" the doctor questioned. Concetta quickly answered and was thankful for someone whom she could understand and could also understand her.

"You will be detained with your son until it is determined if there is a bond posted by someone here in America," stated the physician as he listened to Samuel's heartbeat. Even though Concetta now understood the language he was speaking, she did not understand what he was saying. What did he mean, detained?

Concetta and Samuel were escorted down a long, bright white hallway by a rude, cold woman in a white, rigorously starched dress. She wore heavy stockings with a perfect seam up the back of her thin calf. The woman was silent and merely gave a twist of her wrist in a gesture for Concetta to enter a small room at the end of the hall. She stepped in with timid, dimming hope and found herself in a small, cement block room with a lonely, tiny window facing the ocean. A sagging, iron spring bed boasted the only furniture in the room. The mattress exhibited stains and smelled of mold and urine. Despite the condition of the bed, the brightness of the white walls was soothing to Concetta as it was quite an improvement from the dark, dingy hull of the ship. She could hear the noise of the pier and the occasional splash of the seawater upon the rocks at the shore while being entranced by seagulls as they effortlessly soared overhead. Before Concetta could turn and thank the woman in the white dress, the door to the little room closed. It was all so frightening and confusing, but God would watch over them, just as her father Giovanni had said.

Concetta set down her parcel and tried to show Samuel the harbor. They were both exhausted, and Samuel soon fell asleep on the meager mattress. Concetta watched the moon rise through the tiny window overlooking the water and took comfort in knowing her dear mother's and father's eyes fell upon the same moon. As she gazed down at Samuel, such a happy little boy, she knew his grandparents would certainly be proud of how well he had made such a difficult journey.

"We've come all this way; surely we will be able to stay in America," Concetta said to herself. Concetta felt great uncertainty, as she did not know if this seclusion was permanent or temporary. She and her son were now at the mercy of Ellis Island and its immigration service.

Sleep came easy to the two exhausted travelers regardless of the meager conditions. They were exhausted in every way and had fully surrendered to sleep.

Concetta was awakened by voices speaking in the hallway outside her door. At first, confusion filled her thoughts. Where were they? There was no way to know what time it was, as her concept of time had drifted off on the breeze that puffed through the tiny window. A kind, elderly, English-speaking gentleman came to their room carrying two bowls of rice, a small loaf of bread, a pitcher of water, and a soft smile of acceptance. He walked with a slight limp and spoke very little. He placed the tray of sustenance on the edge of the bed with a soft smile and motioned for Concetta to eat. She was grateful to the man for bringing the tray, however scant the portion.

Concetta lost count of the days this kind man brought them their daily food. Keeping track of the days was equally as difficult here as it had been on the ship. Twice a day the gentleman would appear at the doorway, offering the same meal. Although he wasn't much for conversation, she once overheard him arguing with one of the men. Probably the man she remembered who wore his hat in the building. Concetta laughed. She wasn't sure what the two men were arguing about, but it appeared the older man was preventing the younger man from trying to enter her room. She never understood this older gentleman's words, but the care he put into his soft-spoken tone was unmistakably kind and soothing. His compassion was well received as

Concetta was starved for some compassion and kindness after such a horrific journey that, at the moment, she completely regretted.

On what turned out to be the fourth morning of seclusion from the new world, Concetta once again heard the footsteps of the kind Englishman. However, when the door opened this time, in stepped a familiar face. It was Mike Tassone! Concetta leapt to her feet as though guided with puppeteer strings and hugged him uncontrollably. He spoke Italian to her in familiar, soft, comforting words, and she was saved at last. Tears of gratitude streamed from her beautiful dark eyes at the sight of a familiar face. She remembered Mike as a member of her little village in Calabria. He had been one of the first Calabrian men to leave their village and journey to America. Mike's wife and children were still back in Calabria. Concetta was told that he went to America to strike it rich and would then send for his family. That had been more than seven years prior. Concetta couldn't think about that now. All she could manage was to lean all her trust on a familiar friend. Mike continued to console Concetta, who cried with rejoicing for most of that day.

As they exited the area of Ellis Island, Concetta turned to look back at the long lines and questionable treatment she witnessed there. Once again, she pulled Samuel close and hugged him, thanking God they were finally on their way to what would become their new home. Once again, the now trio found themselves on the waters edge. Another ferry loading. Lines and lines, always lines. Concetta turned to Mike with great concern in her heart.

"How long will we be detained on this ferry?" Concetta questioned Mike.

"Not to worry my dear, this is the ferry to the mainland. Very soon we will in New York City," replied Mike.

What a sense of relief for Concetta. Perhaps now she could let down her guard a bit. Mike was right, just a short journey across the water and they were disembarking once again. Samuel was so excited and couldn't help but shout out at the sights before him. Mike lead the way up the pier and past hundreds of immigrants. The air was filled with voices of gratitude, anxiety and fatigue. Also adrift on the air was the promise of a better tomorrow. The sensation of opportunities and exciting challenge was palpable amidst the crowd.

Three

Mike took little Samuel into his arms, hoisting him up on the buckboard of the horse-drawn wagon. He then extended a hand to Concetta so she could climb aboard. As the horses proceeded forward, Mike explained that Francesco had been anxious to see Concetta, although he was painfully aware and slightly concerned at the prospect of Samuel. Mike was certain that Francesco was unaware that Concetta had a small child. He did not share his brief concern with Concetta, as he expected that Francesco would more than likely be tolerant of the fact, as he'd been so tolerant of many issues.

The regular clopping of the horses' hooves was hypnotic. Concetta began to ponder the hardships of the journey across the sea. The heartbreak of potentially never seeing her mother's beautiful, flawless face or her father's rough, worn hands, created from working so many years in the olive tree fields, was overwhelming. A salty tear slowly trickled down her cheek despite her fighting back the emotion. Mike looked at Concetta and boldly offered, "It is best to leave your memories with the sea. There is a hard journey of life ahead of you. Do not be held back by your memories. You must only look forward now."

Concetta wiped away the tear from her tanned face, for she had to face the realization that Mike was right. It was then she promised herself not to speak of the past and to always look forward. It was necessary for Samuel. This was his country, the place he would make memories to cherish. She would not allow herself to anchor him to a memory of the past. As any mother would, she wanted him to look to the future. *Maybe conversation would help*, Concetta thought to herself.

"No Francesco?" Concetta questioned. Had he changed his mind? What would she possibly do if he had? The thought of having to return to Italy, while appealing at this moment, meant getting back aboard a ship. A fate unwelcome to Concetta, even in theory. When would all these questions stop? Why was she so unsure of herself? What had she done?

"What? You are disappointed to see me?" Mike jested. Mike's reply was simple and logical. "Francesco works very hard for the Zinc Works in New Jersey. It would be impossible for him to find the time to make a journey to New York. That is why he has sent me in his place."

A sheepish smile spread across Concetta's face, and Mike laughed out loud. It was a moment of mercy, of acceptance, belonging, and release, of happiness shuffled into days of anguish.

From that point on, their discussions were lighthearted, and the time passed. In no time at all, the horses seemed to sway to a halt. Another Italian man stepped to the side of the horses and took the bridle of one. Mike jumped to the ground and shook the gentleman's hand.

"This is my friend, Lorenzo," Mike proclaimed. "Lorenzo is the owner of the wagon and horses," he explained to Concetta. "He has helped us a great deal by loaning them to us in order to navigate the city in a timely, safe fashion. Walking from immigration to the train station is very dangerous," he went on.

This comment made Concetta curious, and she wanted to ask more questions, but now was not the time. The train station was loud, bustling, and confusing for an immigrant, and once again, Concetta was grateful to Mike for his ability to distinguish the correct train and platform. Again, everything was in English, and Concetta could not read a word of it. She marveled at Mike's capabilities in maneuvering the process of traveling. Once on board, Mike leaned back on the seat, reached into his coat pocket, and pulled out a shiny red apple. He tossed it from hand to hand and then let it roll down his arm into Samuel's lap.

"There you are, little one," Mike said in a grandfather-like tone. He reached into his knapsack and produced another apple for Concetta. Many years after that moment, Concetta would still consider the apples her greatest gift from a friend. They were beyond hungry. Their stomachs had long forgotten how to cry for food. Small amounts of bread and water had been a staple for three weeks, evolving into bits of rice. The sweetness of the apple and its ripe juices gave them both reason to believe this was indeed the land of sweetness and plenty that would become their home.

In the early 1900s, New Jersey seemed to be in a constant state of confusion and chaos. So many people crammed into such small spaces. Constant noise and odors that were new to Concetta. As the three Italians walked from the train station to the boarding house where Francesco was living, people jeered or mumbled under their breath at them. Concetta could not translate English, but she could feel the sharpness of their words, the coldness of their speech, and the sting of the sentiment. Her beautiful dark eyes looked to Mike with bewilderment. She had never felt the searing of words, in any language.

"Ah, yes, my dear. You won't find the loving arms of the old country here. Stick to your own, my sweet. Try to stay within the Italian community as much as possible. It is there you and little Samuel will be safe and find your new home," cautioned Mike.

"But we have come here to be American, to be part of a community," Concetta retorted.

"It is of no matter. Those who have sharp tongues and evil hearts are not interested in your motives to progress into the future. They exist within their own selfish world and somehow view you as responsible for their own ugliness to others. As though it is we who have blackened their hearts to humanity when in fact it is their fear that has incarcerated them into a tomb of despair and hate," explained Mike.

"Now, we are here," said Mike as he set Concetta's small bag on the limestone step. As Concetta looked up, her eyes were wide with wonder.

From a third-floor window, Francesco spotted the trio and was elated. He bounded down the three flights of stairs. He gave no mind to the echo of his footfalls on the steps as the stairwell was already filled with the noises of daily life. Mrs. O'Neill was still arguing with her husband, the Coolidge family's baby was still crying, and the large Rizzo family must've been having a loud gathering. As Mike approached the door, Francesco turned the brass knob and opened the large walnut door.

"Mike! My friend!" Francesco shouted as the two men embraced one another. "Thank you for seeing to this matter for me," Francesco said with gratitude.

Mike stepped aside and gestured to Concetta to come forward. Concetta could feel her heart pounding. Her hands were cold and clammy. Part of her held excitement, and part of her was trying to keep down the apple she had eaten on the train. Concetta leaned over to Samuel and caressingly picked him up. She stroked his dark hair and kissed his forehead. Now, another step forward would transfer them into their new life together. Concetta carefully climbed the five stone steps until she reached the doorway. With each step she was sure her ankles would break beneath the weight of her fears and anxiety. They did not. She reached Francesco.

He reached out to her with both arms on hers, took a moment to take a good look at her, and then pulled her close to him in a tight embrace. He kissed her on the cheek and barely whispered, "Thank you for coming."

Once inside the little third-floor apartment, Concetta began to allow herself a feeling of safety. She slid Samuel down her body to stand on the wood floor. It felt like the first time she had released him from her arms in more than a month. Samuel promptly ran to the window to see his new view of the new world. His eyes were wide as he absorbed the scene that couldn't have been more different than where he came from. Instead of rolling hills and blooming grasses, horse-drawn buggies and pedestrians were moving in all different directions. The noise from the street seemed to gain momentum and volume as it rose up from the sun-warmed cobblestones. Samuel spied an old man carrying a large burlap bag on his shoulder. As their eyes met, the old man gave Samuel a wave and a wink of his eye. It would be a moment that Samuel, even at a very young age, would always remember. Years later, he often thought of what may have happened to that smiling old man who somehow welcomed Samuel with just a wink.

The conversation between the three adult Italians in the apartment was jovial as the men sipped on homemade wine. The two recalled many events they had conquered in the past, and Concetta was content to sit quietly and allow their words to become the song that would signal her survival. It was almost one month ago since she and Samuel had enjoyed the company of laughter, the ease of home, and the warmth of belonging. There were no questions of the journey, no inquiry about how things were in Calabria, and no mention of expectations from anyone. They had all been in Concetta's shoes—an immigrant with only hope filling your pockets and only dreams filling your heart. There was no need to discuss the obvious.

Those first few days in the little third-floor apartment turned into weeks. Concetta had befriended Mrs. Rizzo from the second floor. She was about the same age as Concetta's mother, and it felt so calming to spend time with her. The Rizzo family was large and loud, as were most Italian families. Their laughter and love were contagious. The more you experienced, the more you craved, not unlike a favorite dessert that you just can't eat enough of. How fortunate it was the two women had met. Mrs. Rizzo had come to America ten years prior, and her husband also worked for the New Jersey Zinc Works. She was mother to five sons, all of whom were scattered throughout the city. But on Sundays, they all sat down at Mrs. Rizzo's rectangular table and shared a bountiful meal made with love. Concetta considered Mrs. Rizzo to be a gift from God. Mrs. Rizzo had taken Concetta under her wing and was educating her in the American ways. She introduced Concetta to the methods of shopping in the local markets. American markets were so different from the Italian markets and very different from just picking vegetables from the garden. Mrs. Rizzo also showed Concetta how to magically grow a tomato plant on the fire escape. It wasn't quite the same as the lovely vegetable garden from home, but it would do for now.

Along with getting to know Mrs. Rizzo, Concetta was getting to know Francesco. He was a quiet, driven man who had welcomed her into his life with an open heart. He had also accepted Samuel as his own, caring and teaching him as only a father could. Antonio would be happy they had found a future here. Day-to-day life was pleasing to Concetta. Tending to the needs of Samuel, maintaining a home, and making the meals kept her occupied. On those days when her memory closet door would not stay shut, Mrs. Rizzo was a shoulder of strength for her to lean on. Mrs. Rizzo missed her family and Calabria also.

"Your longing for home will always be with you," Mrs. Rizzo began. "You cannot run from it; the memory will find you even in your happiest times. Keep it stored in the darkest closet of your mind's hiding. You will learn to tend to it like a beautiful, forbidden garden that only you and God can walk."

There was a sadness that came over Concetta each time she thought of her quaint marriage ceremony to Francesco. How her parents would've loved to be present and how Concetta wished they could've been. The sweet little sanctuary in St. Mary's gave a lovely backdrop glow for their exchange of promise. Her parents would've approved whole-heartedly as the Lord was present. Concetta's memory of the ceremony and Mrs. Rizzo's advice sounded so lovely, like a magnificent, enchanted dream, and that was enough.

Francesco would leave every day for the Zinc Works at 6:15 in the morning to return around 5:30 in the evening. In the beginning, the days were painfully long for Concetta, but since becoming so close with Mrs. Rizzo and several other neighbors, Concetta was content to spend the day apart from her husband. She had come to love Francesco, and he returned her affections, grateful to have someone so dear to share in his life. Life wasn't just about learning to love each other but how to build a future together.

The young family of immigrants spent their first winter together in the little third-floor flat on Wilson Street. Winters in New Jersey were quite a different experience for Concetta than Calabrian winters had been. The winds blew cold, frigid air, and the sun did not shine for days at a time. Keeping the fire going was just another daily task for Concetta. Samuel was getting bigger now and was a great help watching the fire's need for wood. The wood needed to be bought and carried up the three flights. Most days, Francesco would arrive home with an armful of perfectly cut logs.

Looking back, she would remember it as a hard time, but while living it, she was content to be inside and safe from the outside world that was rarely welcoming. Concetta spent her days caring for Samuel and cooking. Concetta was an excellent cook, but ingredients were difficult to find. Mrs. Rizzo had a few secret substitutions for traditional ingredients that could not be found in America. Concetta so missed the fresh vegetables of summer. In truth, there wasn't much about a Calabrian summer Concetta didn't miss. Or much about Calabria she didn't miss, for that matter. Many times, she talked to God about the little stone cottage on the hill, with its bountiful garden and lovely lemon trees. It was during these conversations she allowed herself to picture her beautiful mother and handsome father. It was then—and only then—her memories slid down her cheeks. At times, Concetta would consider discussing a delightful memory with Samuel. She so wanted him to have lovely memories of his grandmother and grandfather. Once, she even opened her mouth to speak and then realized the memories may cause sadness for Samuel, so she retreated the thought. When they earned enough money to return to Calabria, she would revisit the memories with him.

Four

One brisk March afternoon, Francesco returned home from work to find Concetta and Samuel dancing in their makeshift parlor, singing Italian songs, looking so happy and carefree. Francesco stopped to absorb this cherished moment. It made his heart sing to see the happiness flourishing despite their struggles and meager existence. Oh, how he hoped his news would not spoil the progress on the journey through their new life.

Concetta noticed Francesco and smiled. Her teeth were like polished pearls against her dark complexion, and he found her beauty breathtaking. His trance was broken by Samuel jumping up against Francesco's leg. He swung Samuel into the air and up on his shoulders.

"How's my little man today?" Francesco jested.

"Papa, Mrs. Rizzo found a Victrola today, and she let us listen!" shouted an excited Samuel.

"We've been dancing and singing all day," confirmed Concetta.

Francesco set Samuel down and patted his head. He knew the value of happiness and the need to find it wherever one could these days. Whatever they had to face in the future, Francesco knew they would be alright and happy together.

After enjoying a delicious meal, Francesco asked Concetta to sit with him for a while. It was nearly Samuel's bedtime, so Concetta quickly prepared him for bed and lay him down alongside a small quilt made by her dear mother. It was one of the few items she carried across the sea with them. Each time she gently placed it across Samuel's body, she could sense her mother's arms reaching out across that same sea to warm and caress the child. It was the love beneath the stitching that truly warmed her heart and carried with it the protection of angels. A kiss goodnight and one last song before the moon would close the day for mother and son.

As Concetta sat cautiously down next to Francesco, she wondered what the topic would be this time. So often in her young life when anyone asked to have a talk, it meant something was about to change. Lately, the change was not for the better.

"Are you happy here in America, Concetta?" began Francesco.

"Yes, I am happy here in America," she replied repetitively to convince herself of such.

"This pleases me very much, as I, too, am very happy with our family," Francesco admitted. "However, there is so much more I want for us," he continued.

"I would like us to discuss a new adventure," Francesco introduced as he extended his hand to cup Concetta's.

"I'm listening," Concetta said with guarded optimism. She felt fortunate that her husband discussed changes with her. Most wives were not involved at all in any decision-making. Francesco was not like the other husbands in that regard. He felt family decisions should be talked about before making a choice.

"It would seem the time has come for us to journey farther into this vast land that is America," explained Francesco.

"I do not understand," Concetta replied, now with an element of dread in her voice.

"My company expanded to a part of the country called the Midwest. I have been there before," began Francesco. "We would travel by train for two to three days. In Chicago we would then board another train and travel north into the area called Wisconsin. I have made this journey in the past, as the Zinc Works has been planning this expansion for quite some time. This is where we would make our home, Concetta, our permanent home. It is very remote and somewhat desolate, but the hills are rolling and would remind you of Calabria. We could live away from the crowds of people with their jeering tone and the chaos of the city. You could have your own garden, and Samuel would have a yard of his own to play in. However, if this prospect concerns you, I have a sister in Chicago. Perhaps we could make an arrangement with her if that would be of assistance to you to adjust more slowly. Chicago is much like here in New Jersey, very busy and alive with motion. The train runs twice a week from Chicago to the little town where we could live. We can make this a slow adjustment for you if needed."

Concetta was completely silent. Her words were lost amongst her thoughts of tearing away again. Her lips parted as if to respond. Instead, they quivered with disbelief. What had just happened? When was it determined they needed to look elsewhere to live? How had she missed the fact that THIS was not their forever home? She scanned the room as though taking it in for the first time. Its cracked walls warm with echoes of their new life together. Its floors held gouges of tear-soaked boards from Concetta's first days here as her heart wept. Then Concetta's mind came full circle and thought about Mrs. Rizzo. Oh no! How could she part from Mrs. Rizzo? She had become her Italian/American mother. It would be like leaving Italy all over again. Her heart began to race as the scars of memory began to bleed again.

Concetta remained silent as Francesco gently brushed aside her concerns as they once again, spilled uncontrollably down her cheeks.

"Oh, my sweet," Francesco spoke tenderly. "It will be alright; we will find our place, and we will find it together."

Concetta smiled her best smile to Francesco as she gave a slight nod. What could she dispute? A woman's place was to support her husband, and Concetta believed this wholeheartedly. Again, she was grateful to be part of the discussion.

Two weeks later the young family found themselves aboard the transcontinental train, heading for Chicago. The train car was crowded with immigrants and smelled of old tobacco. Samuel had once again been rocked to sleep by the motion of the car on the tracks. He lay so angelic on the seat next to Concetta. He had lived many changes in his short years. Concetta reached out and stroked his tufted black hair that shone like licorice. As she leaned her head back on the coach's seat, she studied the terrain out the window. It was early spring, and the fields were just beginning to turn green. Visible, vibrant spring flowers dotted the landscape.

She closed her eyes and allowed herself a memory of Calabria and its glorious spring flowers. They would be in full bloom now. She imagined her mother walking up the path with an armful of beautiful wildflowers at the end of a day working long hours in the warm sun, planting the vegetable garden and tending to its needs. She could see her father surveying the olive groves in his stark white shirt. Just the thought of home was enough to warm her spirit and feed her soul—even if it was just a memory. This time, the memory also triggered the sadness that overcame her upon leaving Mrs. Rizzo. She had meant so much to Concetta those first few months in America, and she believed she meant quite a lot to Mrs. Rizzo as well. So many goodbyes. Was that what life had become? Probably the best advice Mrs. Rizzo gave Concetta was that one day we will say goodbye to everyone we ever know.

"Our journey together is never certain in length, so we must make the best of every moment," she had told Concetta as she wrapped her in a warm embrace. "Only God stays with us forever." Mrs. Rizzo did not shed a tear as she held Concetta's shoulders and looked her directly in the eyes. "We have served each other well in the time we have been given. I will take you with me in my heart and pray for your continued health and well-being," Mrs. Rizzo declared.

Concetta's memory abruptly ended when Francesco quickly stood up. The train had made yet another stop. Another depot in another town.

"I'm going to get off the train here and buy some of those fruits for us," Francesco stated as he pointed out the window to an older man standing near a wooden street cart filled with fruits. Concetta nodded in agreement as she smoothed her fingers over the Madonna pendant that Mrs. Rizzo had given her. They had never gone hungry, and Concetta was so grateful for that. The young family had plenty of bread and sausage for the three-day trip to Chicago, but a fresh piece of fruit was a welcome treat. Francesco quickly made the purchase and reboarded the westward moving train.

The train rolled into the Chicago station just before sunset. It seemed to Concetta that this new world was series after series of long lines, confused tired faces, and unwelcoming commands from the established Americans. This time, however, she relied on Francesco to take the lead; it was just a matter of following him. Francesco spoke minimal English and could converse with almost anyone. Samuel walked along holding Concetta's hand as Francesco carried a small trunk that housed the only belongings they owned. Inside the trunk were their passports, a large crucifix, some clothing, a baptismal gown sewn by the tender hands of Maria, Concetta's mother, and the beautiful blanket for Samuel.

The train platforms were alive with bustling travelers on their way to a destination known only to them. The air was thick and heavy, and the spring thaw allowed the sweat of the concrete to occupy the nasal passages of all who trod upon its surface. A chill rolled up Concetta's spine, cooler than a springtime waterfall, and she pulled her coat tighter at the neck. Here they found themselves starting yet another journey into the unknown. Was coming to America about continuous change? But, she thought, *We are together, and that is enough.*

Meeting Francesco's sister was quite an event. Francesco's family was elated and excited to see him but cautiously welcoming to Concetta. This was not an unfamiliar experience for Concetta since coming to America, but this was the first time Italians had been so cold and distant. Not to say they weren't welcoming to her, but she felt a distinct coolness. Concetta would never learn the reason for their coolness, but Francesco was painfully aware of their cautious distance. Francesco's sister, Victoria, was jovial and kind but still seemed guarded. She prepared glorious meals for them and made the days very comfortable. Samuel was delighted to discover that Victoria also owned a Victrola!

"Mama!" he shouted. "Victoria also has the music!"

This seemed to please Victoria and soften the small family's welcome. Even though Victoria seemed to soften somewhat, Concetta refused to entertain the notion that she would remain in Chicago while Francesco went on to Wisconsin to establish their home. Concetta and Samuel would travel alongside Francesco wherever their journey would take them, no matter the difficulties or time needed.

After about a week in Victoria's home, the little family again found themselves at the train station. This time, their tickets displayed the tiny mining town of Mineral Point. Or what the conductor called "the end of the line." Francesco had to translate the comment to Concetta as she was still unable to understand a word of English. She had been constantly surrounded by Italian-speaking people and, consequently, only spoke Italian.

"End of the line?" Concetta repeated as the train car lurched forward, pulling them to their new home. The sound of metal hitting metal was startling at first, and the noise of the train whistle was piercing. Today they would arrive at their new hometown, their place to love and grow together as a family. It truly was an exciting time! Samuel jumped about from seat to seat, enjoying the gentle rocking of the train. Concetta kept busy monitoring the outside terrain and Samuel's whereabouts. As the city quickly turned into country, Concetta was mesmerized by the landscape. Beautiful rolling hills now green with newness, spring flowers of white, blue, and yellow were so vibrant she was sure she could smell their lovely scent. The occasional limestone formations and moss-covered rocks sent Concetta's memory spiraling back to Calabria. It was times like this her heart was so homesick she could feel the separation of each heart muscle as it continued to beat, despite her longing for home. Concetta would never speak outwardly about her homesickness and frequently thought of Mike Tassone's comment: "It is better left with the sea."

After a gorgeous sightseeing trip through a portion of the Midwest, the train began to slow for another station. This time the station sign read "Mineral Point." Their journey had been so long and eventful since they walked down the sandy path from the charming calm of the little stone cottage in Calabria. Was this the destination? As if an answer from God himself, it was at that moment the conductor belted, "Mineral Point, end of the line!" As Francesco assisted Concetta down from the train, she viewed the turnstile for the locomotive. Indeed, this was the end of the tracks. So many men exiting the train. There were hundreds, all heading for the zinc plant, she suspected.

Suddenly, from behind a puff of smoke, a familiar face once again appeared. It was Mike Tassone! He greeted them with a grand smile and group hug.

"Welcome, my dear friends!" bellowed Mike in his larger-than-life voice.

"Mike is like my guardian angel, my dear," Francesco explained. "He is always willing to extend the arm of friendship and assistance whenever and wherever I need him, even if I don't know I need him."

Apparently, weeks prior to the Nardis' arrival in Mineral Point, Mike was preparing. He had secured a place for them to live and even rallied the Italian neighborhood to organize a welcoming celebration for the couple. The Zinc Works was more than happy to reward Francesco with a raise for relocating his family. It appeared they had arrived where they might belong. Time would tell, but for now, that was enough.

Concetta could smell the aroma of the outdoor oven as they approached their new home. Her heart leapt as the scene came into focus. Several men were seated in wooden chairs around the stove. From the decibel of the laughter, she concluded they had gotten into the wine a bit. They wore faded work clothes, and their tanned, smooth skin resembled her own. Just a few feet away stood a long wooden table adorned with a pale yellow linen tablecloth and mismatched plates. Two large vases filled with lovely blue and white flowers from the late spring bloom transformed the table into a magical retreat. The women were darting about in preparation for the meal. They reminded Concetta of the glowing embers that rise from a fire, sporadically floating and darting from place to place, seemingly unnoticed.

Behind the toils and laughter stood, to her amazement, a stone cottage. It held only a shadow of the traits found at the stone cottage home in Calabria. Still, it was a beginning not unlike the ending she left in Calabria. The crowd was gracious and overwhelming for the trio. After several hours of conversation, food, laughter, and directions to their new acquaintances' homes, Mike made his announcement.

"My beloved friends, let us now gather ourselves and allow our newest arrivals to settle in!" Mike commanded.

Each visitor bid their good nights and promised to always be available for any reason. So many new faces, all of whom had walked a similar path to be granted a place to call home. Concetta hoped she could recount the names of all the lovely people who had extended their warmth. The Nardis learned quickly that this new welcoming community would mirror their own beloved community back in Italy. All the Italian immigrants were consolidated on the south end of town, logistically close to the Zinc Works. Each man could walk to and from work each day, which meant less time away from his family.

Francesco, Concetta, and Samuel began their household in the stone cottage on the south end of town. The cottage made of limestone was mostly dismal and damp inside. Much of the time there was water accumulating in the basement. It featured two rooms and an outdoor toilet. Concetta managed to make this dwelling welcoming and warm. Their first summer in the stone cottage arrived early. The soaring temperatures served as a constant reminder of Calabria for Concetta, and she loved it. The family was grateful for the natural cooling of the limestone during the hottest days, and Concetta was grateful for the many similarities to her Calabrian home. Especially this summer, as Concetta now found herself expecting her second child. When the humidity rose to an uncomfortable level, the cottage smelled of damp earth and stale water. The smell to Concetta, now with a heightened sense of smell due to pregnancy, was far too reminiscent of the odors encountered on the journey aboard the ship to America. Sometimes, out of nowhere, that memory would surface, rearing its ugly black heart, reminding Concetta of the difficult journey she and Samuel had endured. The sour taste of that memory would give way to her memories of a sweet life she knew in Calabria. It was bittersweet, as she didn't think she could ever bring herself to journey back to Italy aboard a ship. These memories would have to be just a sweet dream. She would write to her parents and explain all their challenges but would title them as adventures so that they might keep from worrying. Oh, how Concetta missed her mother and father … yearned for their cradle of comfort.

Francesco busied his summer days at the smelting plant. Long, hot days of exhausting work for little pay. Concetta was accomplishing busy days of gardening, sewing, cooking, and spending many an afternoon under her favorite shady oak tree with the multitudes of other Italian women. The women drew much strength from one another, such a valued strength that each would rank it second only to God. These were women of great conviction, women of power, and women of faith. They were content to eat second at the dining table because they knew, without doubt, it was they who kept the weave of life moving forward in a positive direction. They didn't need validation from anyone on how important they were; they knew it. The men worked hard and provided, but it was indeed the women who provided the intensity to propel the family forward through all obstacles. Even when there was not a way, they created one.

Even though Concetta felt very welcome and safe within the community of Italian working families, she did not feel accepted within the larger community. This was a tiny mining town filled with immigrants and migrant workers, but the disdain for the newest arrivals could be felt upon venturing into the business portion of the town. Even though most of the townspeople were first-generation German, English, or other Europeans, they already considered themselves American and were unwilling to allow other more recent immigrants the same chance they had been afforded, perhaps only a generation ago. This kept the newest influx of immigrants segregated amongst society, and they sought safety within themselves. It was just easier to congregate with "your own kind." This disdaining attitude toward the Italians was especially noted by the men. After all, the women had each other and were content to gather and form community amongst themselves. The men, however, needed to converse and do business with the townspeople.

Most Italian men learned enough English to conduct their needed business, and if they didn't speak or understand English well enough, they would take along a friend who could speak in their stead until they were more skilled in the language. Word of mouth traveled with the speed of wildfire as to which businesses were helpful and patient with immigrants. It did not take Francesco long to learn which businessmen were men of honesty, integrity, and compassion.

This new community was enchanting to Concetta and Francesco. Glorious rolling, green hills burst open on the edges, exposing the familiar limestone rock and its many stone dwellings. If she listened closely enough, Concetta could hear the voices of her mother and father conversing about the olive fields and the rich soil that nurtured the large Italian gardens. The young Italian family began to fall in love with their adopted home despite its challenges, of which there were many.

That first summer in the Midwest came and went quickly. There was so much to learn and establish while preparing for another child. Vito was born in the late fall of 1911. He came into the world much like all first-generation Italians—born at home in a small dwelling and cared for lovingly by a new-world community of strength and perseverance. This child was American. A dream that many had sacrificed and strived to achieve. Francesco and Concetta worked tirelessly to make this new home their own for each other and their two young sons. That was enough.

Five

Life in a tiny mining town was brutal on all immigrants, not just the Italians. There were the unwelcome stares, the hurtful taunting at times, the low wages, the hard work, and the constant reminder of being perceived as different. When the census taker came around, the young family was not considered "white." They had to register as "brown." Brown, of course, meaning less than. Persistence was their virtue in those challenging days.

The Zinc Works had constructed a massive barracks for unmarried new workers or migrant workers to take up lodging. At least two times a week the train horn would sound as it slowly approached the depot, and what seemed like hundreds of men would disembark the train and walk toward the barracks to register for work. Francesco had been inside the barracks on many occasions, but Concetta had never been in there. It wasn't considered the type of place women should frequent, but there were catcalls from the men when the women would journey past. Francesco's description of the barracks to Concetta reminded her of the ship to America. Therefore, she had no desire to even glance inside.

The building was massive, capable of housing hundreds of men. It was a simple structure with long walkways defined by row upon row of bunk beds, an eating area, and a small washroom. There were three outside toilets for hundreds of men to use. Therefore, there was always a line, and sometimes the stench was unbearable. Most of the residents had a chamber pot beneath or near their bunks. This fact certainly added to the ambiance of the barracks. Francesco was grateful he had his own home to return to each evening.

Wintertime was an indoor experience for the Italian women. They did not need to venture out as they had prepared for the cold days ahead during the warmer months. However, daily trips to the outhouse and the pump to get water were still necessary. Women still gathered almost daily despite cold temperatures. Each would have their turn at hosting the growing number of Italian ladies who had journeyed from the homeland. During the winter months, many a day was spent visiting the older ladies who found it challenging to pioneer the heavy snows that fell in the Midwest. This winter, Concetta found her little cottage routinely filled with neighboring Italians checking in on her and Vito. She was not expected to visit other homes with a new baby and small child. They would come to her. Samuel was now a busy six-year-old but could do many chores and assist around their home. Daily life was busy and moving forward at a swirling speed that could only be challenged by the speed of change.

The spring came and brought with it heavy torrential rains. The little cottage's basement would fill with water every time it rained. Concetta and Samuel spent many an hour baling water from the darkness of the makeshift basement. Their efforts were valiant against the dirty water that crept upward, barely touching the bottom board of the shelves Francesco had built to support the bounty of canning done last fall by Concetta. Jar after jar rested on three thick wooden shelves against the dirt walls of the musty basement. The mixture of dirt walls and wooden shelves gave the room an ominous odor, reminiscent of the ship's hull for Concetta. Funny how an aroma can trigger a frightful memory out of nowhere.

Six

In the blink of an eye, three years had passed. Despite daily challenges and the continued problems with their basement filling with water, the immigrant family had blended well with their adopted homeland. Samuel was now eight, nearly nine, Vito was three, and baby Joseph was one. Francesco and Concetta were cultivating a beautiful life for their young family and were happy. Even though Francesco worked very hard for minimal financial gain, he was grateful to have employment. How they prayed for the day when they could afford a bigger home in better condition for their growing family. Francesco knew it was inevitable they would have to seek out a home more manageable for their needs. The existing problem was, who would sell a dwelling such as this to an immigrant? The townspeople certainly wouldn't want any of the "south side" venturing beyond the imaginary border of worthiness. Francesco would just have to keep his eyes open for an opportunity.

Almost as if he were reading the chronological pages of a book, it wasn't long before his concerns became a necessity. That December, Concetta informed Francesco that she was expecting their fourth child. Now the need was much more urgent, but achieving the reality remained just as difficult, despite the need.

Francesco had met Mr. Townsley when they first arrived in Mineral Point. English was a difficult language to speak and even more difficult to understand. The Italians were anxious to be American and learn English, but their strong

Mediterranean accents made their English challenging for the townspeople to understand. Many did not have the patience to communicate and hold a meaningful conversation with the Italian men. Mr. Townsley was a kind, gentle man. His first name was Harry, but all the immigrants referred to him as Mr. Townsley despite his request to call him Harry. Mr. Townsley always used the prefix of Mr. or Mrs. when speaking to immigrants. He respected all individuals the same and felt each deserved his respect equally. In return, this gained him the respect of all in the community. He owned and operated the local general store. He was a tall, thin man with thinning hair and a kind, soft smile. He was welcoming and helpful to all the townspeople, including the new arrivals. Mr. Townsley quickly became a trusted friend to all who knew him.

Francesco had journeyed into town to purchase a small amount of saffron for Concetta to bake his favorite bread. Upon arrival at Mr. Townsley's store, Francesco decided to confide in him that he was in the market to find a larger, more accommodating home for his family. Mr. Townsley put his hand to the top of his head and rubbed back and forth. This gesture seemed odd to Francesco but perhaps it stimulated the thinking process for Mr. Townsley. *Maybe this was why his hair was wearing thin*, Francesco thought with a smile. "Any help in locating such a place would be very much appreciated," said Francesco with gratitude.

"Actually, Francesco, I may know of a place," revealed Mr. Townsley. "Let us give this some time, and we will speak again."

He patted Francesco on the back in a friendly gesture as he gave him the envelope of spice, and the two men parted. Mr. Townsley was a successful businessman who possessed the gift of making people feel happy, calm, and accepted whenever they were around him. He was truly a treasure to the community.

One afternoon, a few days later, as Francesco exited the large gate to the Zinc Works, he noticed Mr. Townsley waiting just beyond the entry. Francesco noticed Mr. Townsley's kind smile while holding his hat so the wind couldn't steal it away into oblivion. The two men approached one another.

Mr. Townsley greeted Francesco with the usual strong handshake and a pat on the shoulder.

"How's the day going, Francesco?" questioned Mr. Townsley.

"It has been a good day, sir," replied Francesco.

"I have some news that you may find intriguing, to say the least," reported Mr. Townsley.

His arm remained on Francesco's shoulder as he drew him in as if comforting him with a warm blanket as they turned and walked together in discussion.

"I have located a larger home just above the railroad tracks." He pointed up the hill beyond the zinc mine. The structure sits above the city and has a wonderful view of the south side. There are seven acres of land for your growing pleasures, and it boasts a smokehouse, large barn, and small apple orchard. Perfect for a favorite young Italian family I know," teased Townsley with a wink.

Even without seeing this property, Francesco's mind began to imagine his beautiful wife tending to a large garden while her olive skin glistened in the summer sun. He could see his boys running through the tall grasses and climbing the trees as they discovered new and challenging mischievous adventures. He shook his head as if to jiggle reality back. For a slight moment, he had forgotten he was an immigrant, forgotten he had to pass through the stigma of being Italian before he could even begin to hope he may be considered the buyer. Then, also lying ahead like some cruel mirror was the fact that this home was something he probably couldn't afford on the meager salary of a blue-collar worker with an ever-expanding family. So many obstacles to climb before even reaching the plateau that could enable him to wish for such magic.

What a magnificent dream to have, Francesco thought as he dismissed the idea that it could ever happen.

"You and I will go together and look at this place … tomorrow morning?" suggested Mr. Townsley.

Francesco could barely manage a nod and a word of agreement in response. He was so emotional at the prospect of such kindness in another human being who would have no personal gain in helping a poor immigrant. "Thanks be to God," Francesco whispered as he continued his journey homeward.

The next morning couldn't come fast enough. Francesco ate a quick breakfast prepared by the lovely Concetta. He washed his face and donned his boots for the journey he hoped would generate results. Francesco didn't own a horse, so the trek would be on foot. He didn't mind walking, as the blue sky was beautiful that spring Saturday morning. The orange centers of the daffodils along the road were as vibrant as hot, seeping lava from Mount Etna, and the scent of lilacs filled the air. A little yellow bird that seemed to follow his steps was singing loudly, leading the way. For a few minutes Francesco allowed his memory to journey back to Italy. Oh, how he missed his homeland and all the familiar beauty within its borders. It must've been the singing of the little bird that allowed him to daydream. A gift, a glimpse of yesterday, rarely afforded to an immigrant by their own internal reasoning compass. The memories were magnetic and dangerous. For some, the force of those memories could pull you into a place you could not recover from. You must give your heart an American beat, which demanded more drive, more energy, and more discipline. There was no time to waste on looking back, and the danger would be from stumbling over the future if your eyes were not facing forward.

Seven

Looking ahead up the hill, Francesco spotted Mr. Townsley and could already see the toothy grin on his face. Townsley proceeded to walk down the dirt road to greet Francesco. The irony of Townsley descending the path to offer a hand to an immigrant was uncanny and not wasted on Francesco. He fully understood the significance of that moment and would speak of it later as an epiphany in his life.

The house was partially made of stone and ingeniously constructed, implementing the side of the hill for an attached cellar. There was an adjoining wooden summer kitchen in desperate need of paint, but it advertised thin linen curtains now blowing in the gentle spring breeze as they beckoned whispered secrets of home. The house was certainly much bigger and better than their current situation. There was the large red barn at the south end of the property. *We could raise a small number of livestock for butchering and keep the boys busy with chores*, thought Francesco. The opportunity to raise and butcher their own meat was only dreamt of in this new world.

As the men walked the property, Francesco couldn't help but notice the little yellow bird that greeted him earlier now showing off a nest in one of the apple trees in the backyard, where he continued to serenade anyone who would listen to his song. Francesco stopped and took just a moment to inhale and absorb the magnitude of this potential dream home that now surrounded him. So much of life had been a struggle, a finality of goodbyes, a secret longing that cannot be understood or smothered, a positive drive through the bloody thorns of life, always being just close enough to see but never to possess. How could this place even be real? Would it be just another impossible dream sent by some evil trickster to demonstrate yet again how it feels to have your nose pressed against the glass? A dream one could entertain but never share in the joy of living it out.

"What is the price?" Francesco uttered to the man who had now joined them in the front yard. The man looked to Townsley, and Townsley nodded as if to say, "Go on."

"I would sell for $700 and not one penny less!" said the man reluctantly. The man made it also known that if it were not for the fact he was relocating to another state before the winter and the friendship he shared with Townsley, he would not consider an immigrant as the buyer, for any price. Francesco wasn't insulted as he had grown accustomed to these reactions or regulations. For what did it matter anyway—$700 may have well been $7 million. Neither was an amount Francesco had access to. As Francesco opened his mouth to formulate his disappointed decline to purchase, Townsley shook the man's hand and said, "We'll get back to you!" The unenthusiastic man gave a wave of his hand, dismissing both visitors, and the meeting was over.

"I have faith in you, Francesco. Your desire for life and simple contentment is refreshing to me. We will work this out together," promised Townsley.

"It is you, my friend, whom I have faith in, but never could I hope to have $700," confessed Francesco.

The men had forged a unique and unlikely friendship that would endure beyond the boundaries of their mortal lives. For had it not been for Harry Townsley, and people like him, who supported and encouraged the immigrants to adopt this new land as their own, this place we call America would be empty of the vibrant spice and flair that weaves the pattern of such amazing interest.

Harry Townsley somehow convinced the owner it would be in his best interest to sell the property to the young Italian family for $700. Before the last of the spring snow of 1913 melted away from the shady backyard of the house on the hill, Francesco and Concetta were overcome with gratitude and longing when Mr. Townsley gave them the news that the little house on the hill could be theirs. Both were enthusiastic about being treated as equals in the community of homeowners but felt a tugging sadness that they would never be able to accumulate $700.

"What's this, long faces?" questioned Townsley. "We have an arrangement, Mr. Nardi. You will put a down payment on this property and can make a manageable payment to me for the remainder until paid."

"We cannot—" began Francesco, but Townsley held up his hand.

"The deal is done, my friend. We will get the particulars ironed out later. Time for you to start packing your things before that new little bundle arrives."

Moving day was a beautiful Saturday in May. The sunrise revealed a lovely tangerine shade that tapped the memory of blood oranges and a vibrant yellow that rivaled the blooming daffodils. Concetta was now eight and a half months pregnant, and fatigue was a constant companion. With much help from the "south side," a lifetime of belongings was relocated to the rock house on the hill, all before noon. Their meager belongings barely covered the wagon floor that pulled their lives up the hill to continue their life's journey. A tremendous feast was composed in the apple orchard, prepared by the local Italian women. Their skill could create a festival of immense proportion within such a short time. The wooden chairs and tables were filled with smiling, gentle individuals. The little yellow bird's joyous song was muffled amongst the laughter and conversation, but he sang on just the same, in cheerful optimism of his happy tenants. As they lay down their exhausted bodies to sleep that evening, it was a dream come true, and for the young Italian family, and that was enough.

Eight

Concetta's fourth pregnancy was as unique as it was long. She had spent many a sleepless night in prayer for her family. Perhaps it was all the changes their family had endured during this pregnancy or that this was her fourth child. At least that's what she told herself. She found herself feeling exhausted and content to remain within the confines of her own yard. Concetta was usually satisfied to stay on the south side of town, as she didn't want to combat the whispers and unwelcome stares of the townspeople, which made her so uncomfortable. Now she was living on the hill where she had a bird's eye view of the south side, which she thoroughly enjoyed. She had a beautiful family, lovely friends, and plenty of God's gifts to share time with. Learning to speak English was difficult and seemingly unnecessary to Concetta. She was perfectly content to speak Italian. It wasn't that she didn't love America; she just loved her family and wasn't sure America loved them. Regardless, she had little use for English words, as all those she knew spoke Italian to one another. It was enough that Francesco and the boys could speak English.

That summer was hot and humid. In her ninth month of pregnancy Concetta was shocked at her lack of interest in anything except sitting beneath the shade tree. Daily chores seemed a monumental task, and she needed frequent breaks. She continued to tend to their few livestock and large garden and prepared meals, but it took all her might. That June morning, she could've slept all day had it not been for the searing pain. The stone house was calm, and the sun was just peeking over the horizon, signaling a new day. Having been through childbirth before, Concetta had no reason to expect anything more than an uneventful birth. But, unbeknown to all, this birth would be so much more. Labor pains were not an unfamiliar sensation for Concetta, but somehow, these pains were so very different. Two days passed while Concetta endured constant discomfort. As if back in the dark hull of that fateful ship, Concetta began to worry for her life and the life of her unborn child. Something was different and felt very wrong. She began to drift in and out of consciousness. Rosa, the self-proclaimed midwife of the neighborhood, was even beginning to show signs of worry. Rosa sent Samuel into town to bring back the doctor. Concetta recalled seeing the doctor walking up the dirt road, which filled her heart with dread.

"There is little I can do," the doctor told Francesco as he stared directly into his eyes. "The child is being born feet first, and Concetta will endure this pain until the child is delivered or she perishes in the attempt. It is also likely the child will die."

Concetta was a strong, brave woman, but this delivery had gripped her like no other. The pain sliced every part of her body like a hot knife until she felt she could not withstand another minute. Francesco never left her side in fearful anguish of what was to come. All through labor, Concetta remained focused and determined to see this through. Suddenly, after what seemed an eternity, Concetta became calm, quiet, and free of pain. Her memory closet opened wide, and there, at the door, stood her beautiful mother. She was as lovely as Concetta remembered, even though she tried to leave the memory with the sea. Concetta's mother spoke no words, only gave a heartfelt caring smile, but somehow Concetta understood. She knew the end of labor was near, and things would be alright regardless of the outcome.

She gripped the worn, faded sheets of the bed, and her eyes went shut tight as a welded drum. She could hear the doctor's voice but didn't understand what he might be saying. There was a communal humming sound from the concert of prayers occurring in the next room via several Italian women. Concetta didn't hear the shout for more help from the doctor; she didn't hear her own screams; she did not hear the chaos of the moment; and she did not hear Francesco asking God to just spare Concetta's life. What Concetta did hear was a vigorously loud cry from her newborn baby girl who was thrust into this world, born feet first and struggling. Despite the difficulties during birth, the baby girl looked perfect. No doubt a gift from heaven above, guided to earth by her sweet grandmother. Concetta was never certain if this was a dream at a moment of altered consciousness or a true apparition of her sweet mother. Neither seemed to matter as the tiny baby girl was handed to Concetta. She had Concetta's pooling dark eyes and curly dark hair. She had a vigorous cry and rosy cheeks. Rosa gazed at mother and child, for she was awestruck at the delivery and voiced her amazement that in all her years, she had never witnessed a live birth in such a way.

"Surely she came directly from God above to endure that delivery and live," Rosa proclaimed.

The doctor and an old Italian woman both cautioned Francesco and Concetta that this type of birth was extremely rare and that most infants could not survive the birth, or they would die days later from complications. Preparations were made for the care of mother and baby to keep them comfortable, and a novena was implemented. A prayer vigil was held around the clock for several days at the little house on the hill. Concetta was exhausted, and rest was prescribed for several days. During this time, Concetta relied on the rhythmic prayers of her community heard from the kitchen. All hours of the day and night she would hear those faithful prayers. Neighbors helped with the boys, the cooking, and the new baby. Francesco would leave for work in the mornings never knowing if his wife and daughter would be there when he returned. The whole community held its breath.

This time, the old Italian woman and the doctor would be wrong. This little one, who would be called Maria, would not develop complications. In fact, little Maria would thrive. Concetta would also eventually recover. There were no infections, no problems with breathing, and no complications whatsoever. No explanation was afforded, for the two had somehow survived the birth seemingly unscathed. It was considered a miracle, and that was enough.

Nine

Little Maria grew quickly and was no doubt the highlight of Francesco's life. He would spot her playing in the yard as he ascended the hill toward home at the end of a long day. The boys were always exploring and running through the orchard, but Maria was content to play quietly while she waited for Papa to come home. Concetta was overjoyed to have a little girl to strengthen and teach. Even at a young age, Maria stood on an unsteady wooden chair helping her mother prepare meals, toddling along in the garden rows, and sharing time, gaining insight with the community of Italian women under the big shade tree. It was all monumental in the development of a young Italian girl. Little Maria was exceptional help when Concetta gave birth to another son, Anthony. Even at a tender age Maria exhibited kindness and caring for her new brother.

Maria grew and flourished during early childhood. Her days with Concetta mirrored those enjoyed with Samuel at the same age in Calabria—especially the time they spent together in the garden. Concetta would marvel at the similarities her dear Francesco had created between their new home and her birth home. The limestone of the house was similar in color and texture. At times, Concetta thought she could see the same rusted outline of Madonna in the cornerstone of this dwelling as was marveled in the last. *A sign that would signify God's approval,* Concetta thought. The large vegetable garden that lay parallel to the road even held the same pattern of vegetables as did the

Calabrian Garden. However, the dirt here in America was black and rich with nutrients. The Calabrian dirt was pale and dry in comparison. Concetta had made sure to tie a tin pie plate to a post for the metal clanging that facilitated mental transportation back to Calabria simply by closing her eyes. Gardening was a challenging and competitive business among the Italians. Each Italian home boasted a large garden that required many hours a day to maintain. Daily toils and the harvest kept the women and children very busy during the growing months. Some days Concetta would gaze out over her garden and remember her father saying, "I wish for you a grand garden in America." This wish had definitely come true, and it made Concetta smile.

Maria was fortunate to enjoy a safe, loving environment of warmth and guidance served up by every member of the new little Italian community. She was adored and supported but not exempt from discipline, which could be served up by any member of the community who felt the necessity. After what seemed as quick as the blink of an eye, it was time for little Maria to attend public school along with her brothers. Maria cried as Concetta and Maria's younger brother Anthony, who was three, accompanied the four children to the base of the hill. Concetta would've walked to the school, but this year she was expecting child number six, which made simple tasks exhausting. Concetta reminded Maria of what a strong girl she was and that all would be well. Maria hadn't been in the town much, but she'd been there enough to know that she felt unwelcome and out of place. Not only was Maria fearful of feeling unwelcome, but she spoke only a few words of English her father and brothers taught her. How could she go to school and be expected to understand? The townspeople spoke so fast when they addressed her. Maria begged and begged her mother not to make her go. Concetta stopped walking and let go of Anthony's hand to focus all her energy on Maria. Concetta crouched down to Maria's level and took her in her arms, holding both shoulders. Her voice was soft and warm but stern as she spoke.

"We are Italian, but we are also American. You must learn the ways and history of our new country, your country, including its language. My dear, you will grow up here, work here, and flourish here. This is your home. You must be educated to understand this home and all it offers to a young girl." Then Concetta hugged her dark-haired, olive-skinned child tightly. Concetta knew there would be difficulties for the first-generation immigrant daughter, just as they had all endured. The heartaches of segregation and taunting remarks no doubt awaited Maria. But the sacrifices would lessen as time went on, just as they had lessened for Concetta and Francesco. Concetta also believed that this child, who had entered the world feet first, survived beyond the odds and could surely survive public education.

Mrs. Potterton met Maria with fixed eyes and what Maria believed to be an unhappy face. Her thin lips were almost pursed as she eyed Maria up and down.

"Can you speak English?" Mrs. Potterton's lips spit out as a gleam of gold showed through from a poorly capped tooth. Maria understood the words *speak* and *English*, so she nodded her head to signal yes to escape any further threat. Surely Mrs. Potterton must've known Maria couldn't speak much English. However, she never asked her that question again. Over the first few weeks of school, Maria slowly learned more and more English. Maria made many new friends and enjoyed playtime with them. Her brothers were always looking out for Maria. They kept a keen eye on her whether she knew it or not. Playtime, or recess, was new to Maria. Italian families did not have a name for this enjoyable pastime. Her struggle to learn more English was worth the effort just to feel a part of something more than family. The other children were kind and accepting of Maria, even when she only understood part of the conversation, perhaps due to her three older brothers, or perhaps not. Either way, after several weeks, Maria was happy to attend school and learn more about America and her new language.

Ten

The days turned into weeks, and the weeks turned into months. Concetta delivered her sixth child. It was another girl, and Maria was ecstatic! How exciting to have a sister! The same group of Italian women gathered in their home during and after the delivery that had been present for Maria's birth. Even though their constant presence was not unusual, especially during birth, Maria sensed something unusual about their behavior. When Anthony was born, the other children were allowed in the bedroom to see their mother and new sibling shortly after delivery. Not this time. There was a lot of activity and chatter. Also, a priest was called to the home to lead the women in prayer. When Maria approached the women to ask about her mother and new baby sister, she could hear crying. The women would just gesture to the rosary and kiss the crucifix, completing another round of prayer as the priest stood to go.

"Please, Father," Maria pleaded. "How is my mother?" The padre looked at the young child and responded. "Your mother will be fine, my child. It is for your new sister we pray. We must look to God now for the answer." He patted her head, turned, and walked through the screen door.

Maria wondered what he had meant by that. When Maria was finally allowed to visit with her mother two days later, tears of joy rained down her mother's cheeks. Maria hugged her mother tightly. Francesco was also at his wife's side, sporting a weary face. Concetta motioned for Maria to sit on the edge of the bed near her. She slowly unwrapped the soft, warm blanket that cradled Maria's new sister. Concetta began to explain to Maria with each unveiling corner of the blanket that her new baby sister was not well. The calmness of Concetta's voice kept Maria from becoming upset as she gazed down at the littlest member of their family. Maria moved closer to the tiny little girl, who now gave a gentle cry without the security of the blanket wrapping her in comfort. Maria's new sister was absolutely beautiful! Maria slipped her finger into the tiny little hand, and the fragile fingers curled around her finger. The baby had all five fingers, all five toes, the same dark eyes as the other children, and a full head of black hair. *What is the problem?* Maria thought.

"She is my sister, and I love her! She looks like the angels!" Maria proclaimed to the world. She didn't seem to mind the bluish color in the baby's lips and nailbeds. It didn't matter that this new baby looked a little different. She was Maria's sister, and that was enough.

"We have her on loan from God, my sweet Maria," Concetta explained. So much of Concetta's life had been about challenges and faith. Eventually, Concetta would have to explain to Maria that this new sister was not like Maria or her brothers. This beautiful little girl the doctor called a blue baby, a term given to babies born with a congenital heart defect, which caused her lovely smooth skin to exhibit a bluish shade. Her tiny nail beds and toes also displayed a chalky blue color. Maria understood some kind of issue created these bluish hues, but today was not the day for explaining. Today Maria met her new sister for the first time, and she was immediately in love with her and her unique beauty.

Six days after being born, the name Nicolena was given to the little girl with steel blue fingernails. She was perfect in every way other than her heart's circulatory system did not function properly. Francesco and Concetta adored the little angel, and her siblings doted on her every whim. She had an angelic face, delicate features, and shining dark hair. Nicolena's personality was like that of a gentle summer breeze: subtle, calming, and pleasant. She would be the youngest child born to Francesco and Concetta. This child would complete their family.

As Nicolena grew, she became even more beautiful. By the time Nicolena was a year old, she was walking and followed Concetta everywhere. Her Mediterranean heritage, merged with the bluish cast of her skin, sometimes made it difficult to detect the abnormality. Often it seemed as though she was not ill at all. The little Italian family was indeed blessed to have her, as she brought joy to every moment. Nicolena was a popular guest during the daily Italian lady meetings. Each mother loved Nicolena, holding her high in their prayers, for they knew time was precious. Nicolena would sing and dance as she paraded through the seated ladies under the big tree in the front yard every afternoon. Heaven had certainly sent a bundle of joy in this special little girl. Nicolena also helped with the chores assigned to her as she grew. She wanted to be a productive part of a family that worked so hard.

Continued hard work and everyday difficulties were a common ritual for the Italian family that lived quietly in the little stone cottage on the hill. All the children worked as hard as their parents to make ends meet for the family, which often fell short of the need. Oldest to youngest were expected to perform at their level of capacity, and they did. Their lives were distanced from, but not that different from, any other American family of the time. Life was about struggle, survival, and gratefulness from one day until the next. World War I was behind the country, and all eyes were focused on the future. This had been the "war to end all wars," so optimism was widespread. Francesco and Concetta were grateful to live in a free nation with their beautiful family.

Although the young immigrants kept their memories of their birth land private, an occasional correspondence from Italy would reach their door. Word was slow in coming, and the news was often several months old. Most updates told sad tales of woes from across the ocean or the loss of someone they held very dear. The letters carried sadness like a plague, spreading their tears and heartbreak from one heart to another. The language of pain requires no interpretation. An ominous letter filled with sadness can have only one reaction, that of extreme despair. One by one, as the letters came with that familiar postmark, Concetta and Francesco learned of the passing of their parents.

These were traumatic times as each had not seen the other in many years. It was difficult to fathom any decline in health amongst their parents. After all, they were vibrant, young, strong people, or at least the last time they saw them they were. The most difficult loss for Concetta was learning that her beautiful, perpetually young-looking mother had died. The words on the stained paper cut through her heart as the light of dawn slices the horizon. Clearly, she was not prepared to say goodbye to her mother. Concetta closed her eyes to weep and pictured her mother, Maria. She could see her all those years ago, waving goodbye in her wispy cotton dress to her young daughter bound for America for what unknowingly would be the last time.

Any dreams of going home now would be in vain. There was nothing and no one left to return to. If only she had known that the day she left would be the last day shared together. How had time slipped so rapidly from her grasp? She had always planned to return to the stone cottage in Italy. She'd played out the scene so many times in her mind; it would be a surprise. She would hug her mother and father so tightly and tell them all about life in America. Concetta would talk about the journey on the boat, their first home in the east, and now their little stone cottage in the rolling green hills in the center of the country. They would sit for hours in the shade of the warm Calabrian sun and then retire to the summer kitchen for the evening of wonderful togetherness and a refreshing glass of lemonade. This beautiful reunion would now indeed remain a dream of the heart. The days at times seemed endless, but the years had rolled by, removing the opportunity for a return to the Calabrian countryside. The sadness and longing for Concetta's parents would remain within her heart always. So many shelves in her memory closet were filled with lovely thoughts and special people who had graced her life's path.

Eleven

Immigrants were resilient and driven forward by the desire to succeed and be happy. They had a strong faith in the legacy of their family and a strong faith in God. It wasn't important that life became easy; it was important that they built a strong foundation for their family, as if planting a large, bountiful garden, knowing that they would never enjoy the fruits of it. However, their families would indeed receive benefits, and that was enough.

Time moved forward, and the family quickly sifted through the 1920s. When the stock market crashed in 1928, it barely made a difference to the little Italian family. The crash made a great difference around town, however. Many families had no access to their money and found themselves without for the first time ever. Money had been scarce to the little Italian family every day in America, and they were accustomed to providing their own food and meager necessities. Concetta was perpetually grateful to God that Francesco had a good job and their family was happy.

Days after hearing of the stock market crash, Nicolena became ill. Time is often a gift we are unaware of until fate reminds us that we are all just travelers on this journey. As the country was amidst the throws of the Depression, Nicolena was fighting her own battle. She suffered from a recurring upper respiratory illness. She would barely recover from a bout with pneumonia before being hurled back into the struggles of yet another illness. Dr.— Springer was a regular visitor to the little house on the hill. The family made sure to compensate the doctor by presenting him a chicken or a smoked pork hind for his kind compassionate care of Nicolena. Somehow, the doctor was able to obtain a small supply of penicillin, a newly discovered miracle cure for many of the sick. Each time the doctor would inject Nicolena with the thick, milky white substance, her symptoms would seem to improve. Indeed, much of the world would benefit from this wonder drug called penicillin, but it could never save Nicolena.

As Concetta had told Maria ten years prior: "We have her on loan from God." The time had come for God to call that loan due. For ten years her struggling heart had fought to circulate life throughout her tiny body. It simply had outworked itself, and Nicolena was tired. Her fatigued small body had exhausted itself, and organs were failing. The congestion was heart failure disguised as a cough. The cough lingered on and off for three years. She was so brave, lighthearted, and giving throughout her short life. It seemed unkind for God to call her back now, but the gift of Nicolena to this world was coming to its completeness. At age thirteen years, Nicolena's loving heart, which taught so many others how to love, exhaustively stopped beating.

Immigrant life had prepared Francesco and Concetta for many realities but losing Nicolena proved to be more than Francesco could bear. Concetta watched helplessly each day as the sparkle that once shown in Francesco's eyes slowly diminished. His own joyful, persevering spirit stolen away by the death of his sweet child—never to return— buried in that lonely, cold part of the cemetery where his beloved youngest child now lay. He remained positive and hardworking for his other children, but more than a piece of Francesco's heart went with Nicolena the day she left this earth, and he would be forever changed.

Concetta also struggled with her grief. She was an indestructible force until this devastating loss. The other children also suffered great sadness. Maria now cared for the house and garden as Concetta could no longer hide her lack of interest in being outside in the sunshine. Nicolena loved the sunshine and the garden, a trait no doubt inherited from her mother. For Concetta, being in the garden without Nicolena was just too painful. Every butterfly or bee reminded Concetta of little Nicolena. Maybe her spirit now lived in one of those beautiful insects? Or the brush of the wind told a secret only Nicolena would know. Nicolena's presence seemed to be everywhere.

It also pained Maria to be in the garden, as she felt the void of giggles and songs from her younger sister. Once, Maria thought she caught a glimpse of Nicolena's smile from behind a tall tomato plant, but it must've been a shadow. Or was it?

Francesco stoked his pipe as he leaned back on the homemade wooden chair next to the large garden and watched Maria pick some fresh basil for their dinner. *Nicolena should be here helping,* he thought. As he sat, his thoughts wandered to another young woman he'd had the pleasure of watching work a garden with her two daughters. Memories of decisions made in the past, not to be revisited now he decided. Francesco had never spoken outwardly of that decision forever left in the past, but he questioned if it held some responsibility in losing Nicolena. Like all things of the past, he immediately shed it from thought. Sadness had filled their little home, and Francesco wondered if there could ever be laughter and happiness again.

At the time, it was not discussed that Nicolena possessed angelic traits almost from birth. Her beauty was simply too overwhelming for this world. Therefore, she was afforded only a short time here on earth. Now she would reside in heaven from where she came, where she was undoubtedly greatly missed. Francesco preferred to think of her residing among the other angels, preparing a place of loveliness and quietly waiting for all to share.

For the mourning immigrant family, dying in their new country proved to be just as difficult as living there. As if losing Nicolena didn't inflict enough distress, the undertaker insisted on the twenty-dollar burial fee before picking up the body for burial. Her final resting place would be at the back of the cemetery, as she couldn't possibly be interred among the deceased Americans. Let us remember, she was born in America but still considered foreign. Francesco had no strength left for this battle. The acceptance of segregation and the loss of dear Nicolena took the fight away from Francesco's heart. He would pay the twenty dollars somehow to ensure Nicolena would have the proper rest in her eternal life. The night of the viewing, every Italian in the area came to the little house on the hill. There were many tears and condolences shared. Many townspeople also arrived to express their sorrow for this great loss. A small red coffee can had been placed on the counter of the summer kitchen and was overflowing, and bills spilled onto the counter. It was a beautiful offering of goodwill from those who had basked in the many joys and gifts graciously given freely by sweet Nicolena. Francesco used this kind gesture of the community to purchase three plots in the local cemetery—one for his dear daughter, one for Concetta, and one for him so they could lie in peace together for all eternity. Such a wonderful community of friends they shared. Somehow, the evening passed, and with the morning, the sun found its way to rise.

Concetta, Francesco, and their beautiful family found themselves inside the small graveyard on the southwest end of town. The freshly overturned dirt now silenced their joy, and Francesco longed to be with Nicolena. The immigrant family had endured and rose above so many hardships. Perhaps it was the tiring of Francesco's soul or maybe the realization of a shortfall in the life he planted in this newly adopted homeland that compounded the loss of Nicolena. All his strife was for his family, of which she was the youngest member—a lovely, caring daughter he could not protect from harm. Francesco and Concetta held each other tight, both understanding the finality of goodbyes, for they had endured many—each tear representing another memory that would require suppression to keep their family moving forward. Francesco looked at his remaining children as the wet dirt scent wafted upward. Samuel, Vito, Joseph, Maria, and Anthony all stood with the same heartache and loss as their parents. All were injured by the absence of their sister. Francesco gathered his emotions, cradled his beloved Concetta, gave Nicolena one last gesture, and guided his family away from the gravesite. They would love Nicolena forever holding her memory close in heart always.

Twelve

The Depression era brought many changes to all of America. Newspapers became pitiful containers for allegedly despairing news spreading rampant across America. Evening radio revealed disturbing acts of self-destruction and thievery. It was as if the gates of hell had opened, and everyone was being vacuumed in. Every day when Francesco crossed the railroad tracks walking to work, there were more vagrant travelers arriving in the little mining town. Some were just riding the train along its way, hopping on and off to pick up odd jobs where they could. Some chose a life of crime and used the railways as a getaway. History would label these men "hobos." Concetta warned her children to stay clear of men such as these, for their intentions were not always kind. A group of transients had constructed a makeshift living area in a wooded spot not far from the tracks, which made it close to the house on the hill. Though most of these men were harmless, Concetta believed in never letting your guard down, and she instructed her children to do the same while still giving a person respect. It wasn't just hobos that were riding the trains.

The end of the line brought an eclectic group of men daily looking for work. Many men were sons, husbands, and fathers. Before the crash, these men held prominent positions in their communities and had the means to own fine homes and cars. Yet, here they were, shoulder to shoulder with those whom they previously viewed as undesirables. Men came by the hundreds on the train, hoping to earn enough to feed themselves or maybe get lucky enough to send home money to their starving families. The traveling men took up residence in the large barracks hall, and they were grateful for the primitive accommodations: a dry place to sleep, a cup of soup, and a wool blanket that itched and scratched with every touch. Humility is a strange and powerful thing, but once you learn it, it remains forever yours.

There was much work to be had within the Zinc Works, but some of these unfortunate fellows brought with them anger and frustration at their current situation. Many had given up hope that their families were still waiting for their return, or they simply could not return and face the reality of abandonment. Alcohol overconsumption was a problem for many. Sadness, despair, close quarters, and alcohol led to many a disagreement in the barracks.

One warm evening, Antonio Bertucci, a mild-mannered friend of Francesco, was summoned to the barracks because a terrible fight had broken out. Antonio was a foreman and a fair man who all respected, especially Francesco. He thought so much of Antonio that he named his fourth son after his good friend, who was more like a brother. When Antonio arrived in the barracks that evening, two men were entangled in a rage-filled argument. It took several minutes to separate them, but finally, Antonio was successful with the help of two other immigrants. As Antonio escorted one combatant to the door of the barracks, the other intoxicated fighter pulled a revolver from his tattered bag sitting next to the bed. Vision blurred, the man pointed the weapon toward the door and fired. In the blink of an angry eye, Antonio, an immigrant father of six children, soon-to-be seven, lay mortally wounded on the barracks floor—the unintended victim of a ridiculous argument over who had damaged a deck of cards. Antonio was the voice of reason and calm; the man who had helped so many in their time of need; the man who remained positive against the most insurmountable odds; the man who now lay motionless as his immigrant, caring soul slowly drained from his body. Another reminder of the harsh reality and desperate times the papers were calling the Depression.

Francesco took the death of Antonio especially hard, maybe because it came on the heels of Nicolena's passing or maybe because there had just been so much heartbreak over the years.

How could this tragedy have happened? Who would care for this man's family now? Francesco thought. Most Italians on the south side could barely care for themselves in this dark time, let alone another family. What they did have was an abundance of love and care for each other. Somehow, they would help Antonio's family. These brave, strong immigrants had each other, they had their wits, and they had unwavering faith in God; to them, that was enough.

Maria was excited to celebrate her fifteenth birthday. Her father had promised her a licorice piece from Mr. Townsley's store. Kind Mr. Townsley was always reaching out to help those less fortunate than he. Of course, it was Mr. Townsley who purchased the house on the hill all those years ago and allowed Francesco and his family to pay him back little by little, of which they paid every penny with tremendous gratitude.

Francesco and Concetta's family, including Samuel and his lovely wife, Vito, Joseph, Anthony, and Mike from across the road, celebrated Maria's birthday at their home. Family times were one of the most special times, and Concetta relished the moments, as did everyone. Nothing was as remarkable as a large Italian family gathering, and they occurred often for many different reasons. Concetta told her family that Italians were fiercely loving and had much love to share and express to one another. That was her rationale for large family gatherings. Whatever the reason, everyone loved them. Francesco brought Maria some candies from Mr. Townsley's store as a gift, which came with a resounding hug from her father. There was laughter, good food, and family to enjoy. No one discussed or thought about the looming Depression outside of the celebration. Whether it be the country's Depression or the personal challenges of each attendee, no one used their time to fear what awaited just outside the party atmosphere. Today was reason to celebrate. Francesco and Concetta's daughter was turning fifteen, and that was enough.

Thirteen

One week later, Concetta collapsed in the yard while walking to the rocking chair under the shade tree. Mrs. Bertucci found Concetta when she arrived for a typical afternoon of fellowship. She rallied the other arriving ladies and sent word for the doctor to come immediately. They managed to arouse Concetta and assist her inside to lie down in her bed. Dr. Springer arrived as quickly as he could, examined her without difficulty, and determined she had suffered a stroke.

"No doubt brought on by the loss of Nicolena," Dr. Springer reported.

"What she needs now is complete rest and no disturbances," ordered the doc.

Francesco was fearful for the first time in his life—fearful of losing Concetta. Francesco knew all too well the devastation that death could wield. His darling Concetta, she had been the one who held him up when he felt like falling. She had been the one who stood by him in every situation. She had been the one who prayed for the strength to persevere. She was the one who traveled across the ocean alone with a young son just to ease his pain. Her life had been extraordinary, and he couldn't imagine his life without her. He thanked God for sparing her life this time.

"We must keep Mama comfortable and unstressed," he told his children.

Fourteen

The oldest three boys all held full-time jobs within the community. Business owners and factories had slowly begun to accept the immigrants as hardworking people who sought nothing more than a happy life. Maria would now have to surrender her days of going to school. She was needed at home to care for her mother and keep up the daily functions of the household. As much as Maria loved school, she obliged her father's wishes to leave school and took her place as the woman of the house, now also caregiver to her mother. Concetta would regain some of her strength, but her strong, unwavering will had been weakened from the stroke and also the great loss of her daughter.

By 1930, Maria had in every way become her mother's caregiver, spending her days caring for her mother's needs, tending their large garden, feeding the small livestock, doing laundry, and cooking. Maria was happy and fulfilled to share warm, sunny afternoons with her mother and the other Italian ladies under that big shade tree. She had inherited a love of the sun and outdoors from her mother. The gathering of Italian women wasn't just a social event— although it was indeed very social—it was a culmination of strength. A symbolic passing of the torch of light, giving power from old to young. The women told stories, shared recipes, offered advice on raising children, and supported each other. Sometimes the support was stern, but supportive nonetheless.

Concetta sat quietly under that big shade tree in the corner of the yard for hours as often as possible. Sometimes she just watched Maria move through the vegetable garden. So many thoughts washed over her mind. As Maria's cotton floral dress swayed back and forth through the rows, Concetta found herself reminiscing. She thought of her own mother tending the garden in Calabria. Oh, how Maria resembled her grandmother, with her dark hair and beautifully tanned skin, especially when she tended the garden. The longer Maria spent in the sun, the more obvious the resemblance became. Sometimes when Concetta woke up after nodding off, she thought Maria was her lovely mother, standing there watching over their bountiful garden, which brought her joy. Concetta would blink to clear her mind and there stood her loving daughter. This brought a smile to Concetta to think of the two of them. How proud her mother, Maria, would've been of her granddaughter and namesake.

Concetta would think about Nicolena on these days as well. What would she have been if allowed to grow up into a young lady like Maria? Would she be like Maria? What would she have done with the gift of a healthy life? Thoughts like this would bring a tear to Concetta, as any mother could appreciate. Concetta's health didn't dictate her sedentary lifestyle; her melancholy heart did. Try as she might to be the family's matriarch, she was now content to allow Maria to slip into that role. Too much of her heart lay buried with her youngest daughter. As days spilled over into months, Concetta became fatigued more easily. Her aging body and mind were slowly succumbing to its wear and the difficult loss of her daughter. The doctor offered a medical explanation of her mind's confusion as a complication of the stroke, but all who knew Concetta attributed her state of mind to the loss of sweet Nicolena.

In the fall of 1931, Concetta suffered another stroke. This time some of her mobility on the left side was affected. Concetta now required some assistance when rising from bed and a small amount of stabilization and guidance when relocating to another area. Most of her journeys were now limited to maneuvering from bed to commode and out to the chair under the shade tree. Her stunning dark hair now exhibited a beautiful, creamy white color, but her deep chocolate eyes still held the beauty of volcanic stone and the wisdom of an accomplished life.

Maria was extremely capable of running the household. She had learned and listened to the methods of managing daily home operations since she was old enough to communicate. She never viewed herself as extraordinary, but history would reveal she indeed was, as was Concetta, in every sense of the word. At this point in Maria's young adult life, she had survived being a breech delivery in a time when that itself was miraculous, she spoke two languages, she had maintained a busy household for the last four years, she kept a family content, she could live a full life from the land and what it gave her. She could also grow and maintain a garden that kept the other Italian families questioning her magical methods.

Maria always had a warm, welcoming smile for all those who graced the door of the little house on the hill. She was kind, considerate, and loving. This made her a most gracious hostess for anyone who graced the threshold of the house on the hill. Her enchanting smile and beautiful dark eyes would insist visitors enjoy a comfortable seat and something to eat. She took excellent care of her aging mother and two of her brothers, who still lived at home. Even though her older siblings lived in their own houses now, they typically visited every day as they lived nearby. Each would check on the potential needs of Maria or their parents and were happy to oblige their requests. A friend of Maria's brothers often accompanied them to their childhood home. They would sit on wooden chairs positioned evenly encircling a well-worn, round table in the kitchen. Somedays, they would spend a substantial amount of time laughing and bragging about topics Maria thought to be frivolous. However, these topics seemed important to the men at that moment. These conversations usually occurred over homemade wine and maybe some sausage with fresh bread. Of course, this would then engage Maria's time as it was expected she would keep the wine jug flowing and the sausage plate full.

Perhaps it was Maria's beautiful skin, her dark pooling eyes, or her kind, welcoming smile that caught his unwanted attention. A much older, married man named Marcello would occasionally accompany Maria's brothers to their house to discuss the mutual pastime of hunting and fishing. Many a Saturday morning he would appear on the lawn under Concetta's favorite shade tree, the tree that Francesco's little yellow bird had nested on all those years ago, and sit patiently for the men to congregate. Marcello's presence always made Maria uncomfortable. She could never put her finger on why. There was no specific reason; maybe it was just her reaction to him. Still, he made her very uncomfortable. At times she could feel his inappropriate stares, his brushing against her without warning, and his lewd comments about her dresses. When Maria would express her dislike for the man to her brothers and father it fell on deaf ears.

"He is only a man, Maria! You are a beautiful young lady. He is old and harmless. He is merely expressing his approval of your beauty," explained Francesco.

Maria had always followed her father's instructions and advice, but it didn't feel right to trust Marcello this time. There was something about him that was extremely unnerving to Maria.

Fifteen

Several weeks passed, and life was busy. So much was changing in the world of the little Italian family, but so much remained the same. Maria and her mother listened to President Roosevelt on a secondhand radio that Francesco purchased from Mr. Townsley so that Concetta could enjoy beautiful music while she dreamt away the day. Concetta and Maria enjoyed the president's words as they were soothing and wonderfully hopeful. That Friday evening, they had stayed up a little later listening to their radio because there was some sort of drought in the west. The voice on the radio told of the dire need for rain in these areas and the hardships the people of the area were suffering.

"We should pray for those poor, unfortunate people," Concetta muttered. Maria agreed wholeheartedly. Concetta truly seemed concerned for the plight of those affected by the perilous drought. Perhaps that was why Concetta was still sleeping at six o'clock that Saturday morning in May. Maria was up at five and made her father and brother their breakfast and sandwiches for their lunch pails. Zinc Works had their employees working six days a week to fulfill the demand for enamel. Antonio, Maria's younger brother, would accompany Francesco from the house until they reached the depot. There, Antonio would offer to assist passengers with their baggage or feed the horses in the stable to make a little extra money. Francesco and Antonio bid Maria farewell for the day as she returned the kitchen to its organized state. Then, she climbed the steps to check on her mother. Concetta lay peacefully asleep in her bed. This made Maria smile because Concetta looked like an enchanted princess. Maria carefully closed the heavy wooden door to let Concetta continue to rest. She quietly stepped around the banister and began descending the stairs.

As the kitchen screen door came into view, Maria saw a man standing there, waving hello to signal his arrival. Maria tried to conceal her disapproval of his presence at her door because it would not be proper to greet a person with the uneasiness Maria felt toward Marcello, yet there he was. Without knocking or permission to enter, this man stood at the threshold of her home!

"Good morning, Maria," said Marcello through the screen.

"Good morning," replied Maria in robotic response.

She stood there with her hand on the wooden edge of the doorframe. At first, she didn't open the door as she felt extremely uneasy at his unusual arrival. "The men are not here," she stated without opening the screen door.

"Oh, yes, yes. I am early," explained Marcello. "Today is a hunting day."

"Father and Antonio have already left for the Zinc Works. I don't think they will be hunting. Perhaps you have the wrong day?" cautioned Maria.

Generally, Maria knew about hunting days ahead of time because the men would expect her to have a lunch packed for them to take along. On this day, there had been no mention of it.

"May I wait in the kitchen?" Marcello requested.

Every inch of her body told her "No," but she didn't want to appear rude or have Marcello tell her father or brothers that she was not hospitable, so she reluctantly pushed open the screen door. As the wood braised across the stone step, it expelled an unpleasant scraping sound. The noise made the hair on Maria's neck stand on end. It was as if the shrill scraping signaled the opening of a dark, evil place. Marcello stepped into the kitchen and sat down at their family table.

There he sat at the same round table where he had so many times before. Despite Maria's disgust at his arrival, as a woman, she knew her obligation to offer him a cup of coffee. She secretly prayed the other men would arrive soon. Maria poured Marcello a cup of hot, black coffee into the well-used mug as she felt his eyes exploring every part of her. His presence made her skin crawl. It was difficult to ascertain if the scent of the yeast reacting in the rising bread dough or Maria's distaste for the company made her a bit nauseated. Maria opened a small window to allow the early morning May breeze to enter gently into the kitchen and cleanse her mind of this unsettling sensation. The air was cool and crisp, but the oven would soon warm the kitchen, so she let the spring breeze spill in. She took a drinking glass and pumped the handle of the water pump until ice-cold water flowed from the depths of the well. As she drank, she felt an overwhelming sense to get away from Marcello.

Where is everyone? she pondered. It certainly wasn't like them to be so tardy, especially for a hunting event. Suddenly, it dawned on her that she hadn't retrieved the hunting bags from the closet upstairs. These were usually carefully laid out the night before the men had a hunting date. Since Maria hadn't known about this trip, and obviously her father and younger brother Antonio weren't going, they made no preparations. She excused herself from the kitchen and was relieved to have a reason to exit the company of Marcello. He could sit alone in the kitchen until whoever else was coming to hunt arrived.

As Maria climbed the ten wooden steps to the upper level of the little stone house, her mind was busy thinking of what kind of lunch she could quickly assemble to pack into each hunting bag. She also was more than a bit disgusted that no one had bothered to advise her of this morning's events. Her mind was preoccupied with her anger at the unknown plan and her unexplained, repulsive view toward Marcello. Even though distracted, she quietly turned the doorknob of the hall closet so as not to wake her dear sleeping mother. Concetta was still resting in her bed at the end of the hall. She was still affected somewhat by what would become known as mini-strokes. Maria felt glad that her mother didn't have to endure the company of Marcello.

Despite her stealth in turning the doorknob, the metal latch of the door and the hinges still creaked with disdain into the quiet morning. Inside the closet, Maria saw the hunting bags nestled to one side of the space. She leaned into the closet toward the bags in an attempt to sling them onto her arm. Focused so intensely on not making a sound, Maria didn't hear the footsteps coming up behind her. She quickly noticed the sensation of falling to the ground as if she had lost her balance. Then she was simultaneously aware that she was being pushed into the closet. Once again, she heard the metal latch slide as the door closed. The closet was dark and filled with blankets, old wool coats, and a few shoeboxes, which made Maria disoriented. The light from the hall was now diminished, making it impossible to see. But Maria didn't need the light to identify who had pushed her and was now pressed against her. She knew by his vial breath that smelled of old tobacco and dental caries. She knew by his scratchy wool shirt as his arms slid down hers. She knew by his lustful comments that he whispered into her ear. Maria tried to push him away, but the small size of the closet made this impossible with the door closed. He was, of course, much bigger and stronger than she. Every part of Maria's body was screaming for help, except her vocal cords. Worried she would disturb her sleeping mother with her screams, she kept quiet. *What could my mother do?* thought Maria. What if she fell while trying to get out of bed? What if the screams startled her, and she had another stroke? Maria couldn't bear to cause her mother pain or more hardship.

"What do you think you are doing?" Maria questioned Marcello.

"Be still. It's not like you don't know what you've been asking for all this time, strutting around just begging for me to notice," Marcello whispered as he took Maria's shoulders and spun her around to face him.

Maria pleaded quietly for Marcello to let her out of the closet, even apologizing for his misreading of her hospitality and nothing more, but her words fell through the cracks of that hardwood floor inside the closet. No one heard her scuffle, no one was there to stop this man from taking what he wanted, and no one was there to save Maria.

Maria struck her head on the doorknob as Marcello forced her body to the floor—the same doorknob she had turned and touched almost every day. Now it had betrayed her and stood as a silent prison guard standing witness to the unthinkable. Maria prayed her mother could not hear the heavy, more rapid breathing of this disgusting, evil man. The closet was small, and Marcello was a big man. She felt suffocated in so many ways. Everything happened so quickly. There was darkness, there was fear, and there was pain. All her wiggling, pushing away, and pleading was in vain. Marcello had no intention of letting her go until he achieved his goal. Maria let her mind focus on an old wool blanket that was losing some of its edging. The coarse thread was slightly unwoven on one edge.

I'll need to fix that blanket, she silently told herself. She became fixated on that imperfection as Marcello violated her to his pleasing.

Suddenly, as if waking from a trance, Maria realized that Marcello was no longer holding her down. She collected herself for a moment and then heard the screen door of the kitchen open and close. She listened as his filthy footsteps walked across the stone path. He walked without a care, without remorse, taking her childhood, her trust in people, and her future with each step. Maria lay motionless on the closet floor, her legs extending outward into the hall now. How could she have been so foolish? She stared at the hunting bags with disdain as if they were somehow responsible for what had just happened. What had just happened? She suddenly felt sick. Nauseated by the scent of old wool, oiled wood, and the lingering stench of Marcello. Now, instead of cries for help, tears rolled through the cracks of the floor. She lay there for an unknown amount of time until she heard the voice of her mother yelling out to her.

"Maria!" called Concetta, oblivious to what had occurred in the closet.

"Yes, Mama. On my way," replied Maria.

Maria pulled her pain-filled body to a stand, still trying to comprehend what had just taken place. Was it real? Could such a nightmare be real? She straightened her dress and smoothed her hair as she exited into the hall and stepped into Concetta's room.

"Are you alright, my dear?" Concetta questioned in her heavily accented voice. "You are looking pale."

"I'm fine, Mama," Maria lied. "Let's get you up and ready for the day."

Maria tried hard to put herself into a normal routine and focus on her mother's needs. Try as she might, the once routine day had now become anything but. Maria relived every step of the horrific event. Why had she believed Marcello when he said he was waiting for the men to go hunting? They had never forgotten to tell her about a hunting morning before. Why didn't she scream out and fight back viciously for her innocence? It was her right, even if she was a woman, and he had no right to do what he had. Why didn't someone tell her this man was evil and couldn't be trusted? Someone didn't have to tell her; she knew this, but someone could've validated her feelings. Her instincts had not failed her; she just failed to listen. Maria was flooded with a mixture of guilt, anger, and dizziness. By the time Concetta was dressed and they slowly descended the wooden steps, Maria was physically ill, and her legs were trembling. She could feel the vomit rising in her throat as she patiently assisted Concetta to the kitchen chair. Maria bolted out of the same squeaking summer kitchen door Marcello had slid through only an hour before. She ran to the outhouse, and she rid herself of the taste of the morning's events. Maria sat on the outhouse floor and wept. She allowed herself only moments to grieve. The work of the day wouldn't do itself, and Maria was very responsible.

Sweet Concetta was very concerned about Maria not feeling well. Maria was not the kind of young woman to be ill. *Perhaps something she ate*, thought Concetta. By the time Maria returned to the kitchen, the rising bread dough was more than ready for the oven. This chore would've been completed by now had it not been for the unfortunate incident. Maria's hands trembled with trauma as they shaped the rounded loaves for the hot, fiery oven. She stirred the coals that were somewhat dwindling due to the delay in baking. However, the heat was still intense and would bake the loaves to a lovely golden brown. Most often, Maria would do several baking projects while the coals were hot in the outdoor oven, but on this day, only the bread would make an appearance. The day was already full.

The gentle spring breeze blowing the cotton curtain, the scent of the fresh bread wafting through the slightly opened window, and the sound of a meadowlark singing on this bright and sunny morning should've echoed a glorious day. However, this was not a glorious day. She could not take in the beauty of the morning, for it was stolen by a man with foul breath, stolen like a cat steals the breath of a newborn babe, quiet and quick. Maria prayed to forget this day.

There sat beautiful Concetta enjoying a cup of hot tea. "Will you come and sit a while with your mother, Maria?" she invited.

"Of course, Mama," Maria replied. She loved Concetta with all her heart and would fulfill any of her wishes. There was time while the bread baked to sit and enjoy a cup of tea. The clock showed nearly 10:45 as Maria took her cup to the table. She kissed Concetta's peppered gray hair and then sat beside her mother.

The two women talked for nearly twenty minutes about various recent events. The change in the price of butter, the influx of migrant workers, and the lovely day God had provided. For a moment, Maria's mouth opened as if to speak. Once again, she expressed no sound. Oh, how she wanted to cry to her mother about the terrible man who had been in their home earlier, but she felt ashamed. How could she feel ashamed in front of her mother, who was loving, accepting, and kind? Surely, Concetta would hold her daughter and console her aching self. But what if not? What if sharing this nightmare with Concetta caused her to experience another stroke? Maria could not endanger Concetta by telling her the details of that dark morning. Maria simply placed her lips together and promised herself she would never speak of the traumatic incident.

In the days ahead, Maria would see Marcello in various places, even in her own home, invited there by her brothers, who knew nothing of the previous altercation. Maria wanted so badly to tell her father or brothers about Marcello, but somehow, as a woman, she knew that they would believe Marcello over her. Maria loathed it when Marcello would laugh and talk with her father as if he were an upstanding, righteous man. *How dare Marcello pretend to endear my family?* she thought. Behaving as though he did nothing wrong when, in fact, he was a despicable, vile individual.

Maria lived in fear for many weeks. Marcello couldn't be trusted. He never approached her again but continued to make her uncomfortable with his unwelcome, wandering eyes and facial expressions as if they shared a lovely secret. How revolting and loathsome. Perhaps she had done something to provoke his advances? Maria knew this to be untrue. She had done nothing to entice the fancies of this married older man. Maria decided her previous decision to be silent was the correct one. No one was going to believe that Marcello was the type of man he was. She would keep her distance from him. She would bury her shame along with the horrifying memory, pretend it never happened, and hope that was enough.

Sixteen

Francesco and Concetta's children were almost all grown up now. The youngest child was almost finished with high school. Maria was responsible for the household, care of her mother, the garden, and all meals. Two of their sons were married and living in their own homes nearby. Only Vito, Anthony, and Maria still lived in the little stone cottage with Francesco and Concetta. The late spring of 1932 was very busy. The married siblings still helped with the workload of the cottage. In turn, Vito, Antonio, and Maria also helped their siblings with daily home operations: planting, maintaining, harvesting. It had been difficult that spring to get the vegetable garden planted due to the abundance of rain in April and May. The apple trees needed spraying and pruning, the grapevines needed tending, and the day-to-day operations had to keep going—all routine labors of love for a close-knit Italian family.

Concetta spent her days mostly resting and reflecting. She did embroidery and a little sewing, but her bulky, stroke-ridden hands didn't work like they once had. She enjoyed afternoon visits with many other Italian ladies who came calling to join in the comradery that was the lifeblood of the Italian woman. Most days, by one o'clock, at least ten or twelve middle-aged Italian women were sitting beneath the big oak tree or inside the little summer kitchen around the table, depending on the weather. Maria would also join the group for dynamic conversation. What a wonderful, fulfilling way to spend time. The topics depended on the time of year. During the spring, most conversations focused on planting their large vegetable gardens and potential hardships regarding the planting. Summer would bring talks of the heat and cures for the plight of some growing vegetables. Of course, fall would usher in the harvest and canning discussions. On a rare occasion, the old country would become the topic until a heartstring broke, and then the topic was rapidly exchanged for a less painful one. The main ingredient in the conversation was the ease of discussion. Women speaking freely to one another without worry of recourse. For all of Maria's life, she would reflect on those gatherings and long for their simplicity and the strength they diffused into each woman present. They were like a delicious stew that marinated within the stories from one another, causing each to be infused with a more delightful flavor for life than before. The collection of women together was the secret ingredient to their unwavering stamina.

By late spring 1932, the large Italian gardens were each planted, and sprouts were starting to appear. The grass on the hill behind the stone cottage had turned a bright kelly green, and everywhere you looked was a frenzy of dandelions. The apple orchard was vivacious with blooming flowers and succulent scents. The little cottage on the hill was more beautiful than a postcard, and gratefulness abounded within the little family. On those breathtaking spring days, no one could have known what was looming quietly beneath the visible contentment. However, soon an upheaval would occur on the south side.

Seventeen

It was a charming June morning as Mrs. Romano marched up the hill toward the stone cottage. Maria and Concetta could see her coming from a distance with her determined walk. As she held her skirt up to make the climb, her dark stockings seemed like railroad ties that stood on end, hammering themselves into the hill.

"Does she ever not march wherever she goes?" Maria questioned her mother.

"Now, Maria, she is a kind, well-meaning woman," corrected the considerate Concetta as Maria smiled.

Mrs. Romano started screeching even before her foot brushed the stone walkway that outlined the path to the little summer kitchen. You couldn't help but notice her dark, pointed shoes as she stepped off the walk to join the ladies under the oak tree. Maria smiled again realizing what a character Mrs. Romano was.

"Did you hear the racket last night?" shouted Mrs. Romano.

"No, we didn't," replied Maria as she adjusted Concetta's light shawl around her shoulders. Concetta lightly patted Maria's hand to console her disdain for gossip that was no doubt about to be presented.

"What a beautiful morning, Mrs. Romano. Won't you sit down and share a cup of coffee?" requested Concetta, hoping to redirect the conversation. She wasn't much for gossip. It always involved someone's misfortune, and Concetta had experienced too much of her own to take delight in the misfortune of another. She and Maria saw no benefit in participating in the sorrowful event of someone's woes.

Maria poured Mrs. Romano a cup of coffee and offered her an anise cookie. The three women rocked back and forth in the old metal rockers that had been painted several times over. This year they sported a bright green color, like the lawn mower handle. The chairs were probably as old as Maria and every bit as dependable. They were rescued from the dump and repurposed as yard rockers for all the Italian ladies to congregate their thoughts and considerations. These rockers had stood as a silent witness for many a discussion between young and old Italian women. From the quiet young lady learning about living to the wise old sage who held the answer. Concetta and Maria loved these old chairs for that very reason. They served as a familiar comfort, a constant source of pleasure, and safe dwelling place in an ever-changing, chaotic world.

"So, Mrs. Romano, I can see you are bursting. Tell us about the 'racket' you described," beckoned Maria. Although Maria didn't enjoy gossip, she did enjoy watching Mrs. Romano's eyes enlarge whenever she told a story, especially if she thought no one knew it yet!

"Well, now that I've caught my breath, and not to be spreading rumors or anything, but apparently, Roy Antoine caught his wife with another man last night. He left their home and returned a bit later with a shotgun! Old Roy shot his wife and her lover through the bedroom window! Killed the man on the spot and darn near killed his wife too!" reported Mrs. Romano as she sat back in the rocker, relieved of the burden of reporting.

This information was not like the usual story brought forth by Mrs. Romano. This was serious and terrifying.

"Oh, my goodness!" shrieked Maria as Concetta raised her palm to her face in disbelief.

"That's not all. No one has found Roy yet! The authorities have been looking everywhere for him but to no avail!" said Mrs. Romano exposing nearly all the whites of her eyes. Then she leaned forward, lowered her voice as if the birds in the trees may be listening, and whispered, "I'd imagine he's hiding in that old mine shack of his, probably drinking. I wonder if anyone's checked there!"

"And what of Mrs. Antoine?" questioned Concetta.

"Well, I'm not for certain, but the doc has been at their place all night," touted Mrs. Romano.

Maria and Concetta were both very upset by this development. What a tragedy for this community and family. Now the uncertainty of Roy running loose around the area with a shotgun and nothing left to lose.

"I always knew there was something not to be trusted about that Mrs. Antoine," bragged Mrs. Ramano. "Why, poor Roy had his hands full with her," she continued as she dipped her anise cookie into the coffee.

Why was it always the woman's fault? Maria wondered. She knew Mrs. Antoine from church, and she seemed like a sweet, timid young lady. Maria felt remorse that the poor woman may be suffering.

The women continued to rock back and forth, processing what Mrs. Romano was reporting. Concetta thought of all the social injustices immigrants had endured throughout the years. Perhaps it was the reality of those stresses that had contributed to some of this type of behavior and violence. It didn't make it right, but it could've been a contributor.

Maria also quietly thought about the severity and sadness of the crime. At first consideration, she also wondered what brings an otherwise civilized person to act out this way. Maria recalled so many instances where anger and isolation had taken their toll on folks. So sad that Mr. Antoine was capable of such violence. Maria had seen him many times around the south side of town. He was quiet and polite and gave no indication of a personality that would take a life. Suddenly, Maria's memory drifted back to the dark little closet and Marcello. How she wished she were brave enough to confront Marcello in the manner Antoine did. Perhaps now she could understand a moment of rage aimed toward someone who had deeply wronged another.

What might she have done if there had been a rifle in that closet instead of just blankets and hunting bags?

Anger and rage seemed to be a part of life within the community. Concetta, Maria, and Mrs. Romano talked away the hours, remembering several domestic problems of the past.

"Remember poor old Mrs. Hanny?" Mrs. Romano questioned, "and how her miserable husband pushed her into the hot coal stove in her nightgown, igniting the thin cotton of the gown. Poor dear almost burned alive."

It might have been better if she had, considering the amount of pain and suffering she endured. Living out her days in constant discomfort and disfigurement, both visible and invisible. While Mr. Hanny just went about his daily routines without reprimand. Sadly, there were other examples of cruelty. Concetta recalled the time when widow Lombardi's husband was still alive. He'd been all over town that afternoon, drinking away his alleged sorrows. Upon arriving home, he became so angry with Mrs. Lombardi, for some unknown reason, that he ran over all the chickens in the yard with his little truck—every last hysterical chicken. Then he proceeded to beat Mrs. Lombardi violently until she lost consciousness. He left her in the front yard next to the dead chickens. If the neighbor hadn't intervened in the beating, folks said he would've beaten her to death. A few weeks after that, Mr. Lombardi mysteriously died. No one ever asked any questions of Mrs. Lombardi or anyone else as to the cause of his death. She had survived an unimaginable existence with him, and folks were simply happy that her suffering was over.

There were those few who felt they had no choice but to take matters of a bad situation into their own hands, like Antoine had. Mrs. Romano reminded the women about Mrs. Moretti, who had told the tale that she had a "cure" for a bad husband. Her recipe was guaranteed to improve the temperament of a cruel man. Mrs. Romano jested in copycat style, pointing her finger and stating, "A little rat poison in the hamburger will cure a bad temperament." In Maria's young mind, she now wondered if perhaps this joke wasn't an actual reality in some households. What else could a poor woman do to escape the torment of a brutal husband? All three women found themselves laughing over the prospect of their unusual, sinister thinking. It was nearly lunchtime by now. Maria excused herself to begin making the lunch. Mrs. Romano and Concetta continued to move the metal rockers back and forth as if they generated the thinking process for the women.

Maria smiled at the sight of them slowly oscillating back and forth under that old familiar tree. Two aging Italian beauties just absorbing the beauty of the morning. They deserve to savor enjoyment after the trials they both had endured. Oh, how she loved seeing people happy.

Roy Antoine was eventually found along the flowering path to the lead mine amidst the late spring blossoms of white, yellow, and purple that returned each year to beautify the surrounding hills. Roy had paused near the running stream, where a large oak stump stood prominently, signifying the remains of a towering, aged tree that had succumbed to a terrible lightning storm. Roy Antoine had taken his own life with the very weapon he'd ended a stranger's life and attempted to end his wife's. The scene was such a metaphor for Roy's life; the story gave Maria goosebumps, and the whole town was now abuzz with their version of what happened. Roy's life had been, in every way, parallel with that mighty oak. Antoine had stood strong and brave against the odds all along life's path, and then one day, it was just over, ending with a violent striking blow.

The metaphor of the mighty oak compared to Antoine's life impacted Maria and her thoughts moving forward. All lives met with challenge, diversity, and sometimes heartbreak, but it was perseverance that mattered. On this day, Maria decided that no matter what obstacles life had in store for her, she would stay strong like that mighty oak had been. She would strive to tower above adversity and meet those challenges head-on with solutions. She would not surrender until that final striking blow. Had it not been for the murderous rampage of Roy Antoine, Maria may have never seen the importance of standing strong through a storm. She may never have understood that some things are inevitable and should not be questioned but learned from. Who was she to pass judgment? Immigrant life was difficult enough, but what she had learned about life so far, was to never assume to understand the ways in which others navigated their life path. Concetta and Francesco had taught their children well in the art of empathy. Concetta also taught her daughter how to be a strong woman. Little did any one of the three women know the monumental test of strength that lay ahead for Maria.

Eighteen

The eight apple trees that formed the orchard were in full bloom that late spring morning. Maria loved walking through the orchard with its snow-white blossoms and fragrant scent. The world was renewing itself, and it was glorious. On this day, Maria set out to pick dandelions. This leafy, nutritious plant had become a spring staple in their diet. Everyone enjoyed the sweet, earthy flavor so familiar to spring. Concetta would add a small amount of leftover potatoes to the greens, fresh cut onion, and then sprinkle with a little red pepper. Maria learned at a young age how to pick and prepare these adored greens. They would be a welcome dish at the dinner table while celebrating Maria's upcoming birthday. However, it was quite time-consuming to collect the plant. An entire bushel of fresh-picked dandelions would only yield about eight ten-ounce containers after cleaning and blanching. Maria didn't mind the lengthy collection process; it was another opportunity to spend time outdoors. Maria had inherited Concetta's love of the outdoors from an early age. Mother and daughter would journey together, loving their time spent outdoors in the sun, sharing and being part of the glory of nature. Oftentimes, Concetta would share memories of walking in Calabria with Maria. Oh, how Maria loved the happiness her mother expressed while reminiscing. It was a time of free-thinking, daydreaming bliss, and now memories of walks with her mother.

Concetta was a joy to Maria but also a labor of love to keep her relaxed and calm. Poor Concetta had suffered at least two strokes, and the doctor had informed the family she must be kept calm. Most household tasks befell to Maria, for which she gladly accepted responsibility. Maria loved Concetta with all her heart and couldn't bear the thought of her having another stroke. How do you repay the gratitude you have to a mother? Giving back what a mother gives to a child is an unobtainable goal. It must be paid forward when the child becomes a mother.

As Maria hummed along, digging dandelions, she couldn't help but notice the brilliant yellow flowers that now adorned most of the late-season plants. *Such a beautiful color*, she thought as she snipped them from the plant. Of course, in Maria's home, the blooms were not meant to be eaten.

"Rightfully so," Maria spoke out loud. "Something so beautiful should not be considered food."

Despite being told repeatedly that a dandelion was a weed, Maria felt that the yellow in their vibrant flower was rivaled only by the sun, and that made her smile. She collected a bouquet of them along with her bushel of dandelions.

Maybe it was the sun that shone down that morning, casting its shadows along Maria's path. Perhaps it was the air that smelled of fresh, turned earth and musty leaves. Maybe it was that Maria hadn't eaten any breakfast even though she had prepared a wonderful meal for Concetta and Francesco that morning. Whatever the reason, Maria began to feel dizzy and weak. This had been a long, busy week for the little family. She had not felt her best in many days, but there was so much to do, and she was understandably tired. She was probably working too hard, overly concerned for her mother, or perhaps just not sleeping well. Maria reassured herself these reasons were to blame for her fatigue. It was concerning that Francesco had commented that Maria looked pale at the dinner table a few days ago. He told his daughter she took on too much. *Perhaps Papa was right*, she thought. Maria decided to sit a moment along the path to allow the dizziness to pass while taking in more of the day's glory.

Maria tenderly set the bushel of dandelions down. They were spilling over the edge of the basket, indicating a successful morning collection. She smiled as she likened their appearance to the tentacles of an octopus reaching to attempt to escape from an overfilled market tub. Maria had never seen an octopus, but her mother once showed her a drawing in a book they had borrowed from a Jewish neighbor. The trailing dandelions seemed to hold properties similar to the octopus's tentacles. Maria closed her eyes to try and envision what the market must've been like for Concetta when she was Maria's age. Maria felt her eyes close, and the brilliant light that illuminated her eyelids began to fade. As Maria began to lose consciousness, her body allowed itself to gently roll back onto the cushion of the thick grass. There she lay motionless alongside the bushel basket, brimming with her work. A small bouquet of brilliant yellow dandelion flowers still clutched tightly in her left hand.

Maria didn't hear the singing of "Crazy Joe" as he rounded the corner with his favorite hunting dog, Saul. Crazy Joe was an Italian immigrant who also lived on the south side of town. Crazy Joe had earned his nickname by his bizarre behavior. To begin with, Joe always traveled on foot but used the railroad tracks as a makeshift sidewalk. They were his path of choice. He rarely spoke to anyone unless it was to scold them about an issue or infraction Joe found offensive. Even then, he spoke in Italian. He would continually curse the Blessed Virgin Mary many times on his journeys up and down the tracks. When he wasn't cursing, he was singing. No one knew what each day would bring for Joe, but the good part was you just had to listen to his mantra and then get out of his way. This morning, to Maria's good fortune, Joe was singing. His dog, Saul, traveled a bit in front of Joe, sniffing along and enjoying the morning. It didn't take long for Saul's keen eyes to spy Maria. Saul ran to Maria's peaceful body and began licking her face. Slowly, Maria began to reorient herself to time and place. By the time Maria realized her location, Crazy Joe was standing over her.

"What's wrong with you, girl?" Joe questioned in a tone filled with accusation.

"Oh, gosh! I think that perhaps the heat got to me," replied Maria.

"Heat? It's but seventy degrees out. No such thing as too hot in this land. Come on now. I'm gonna take you to your papa." Joe stated in an inconvenienced voice.

Crazy Joe didn't help Maria to her feet, he didn't pick up the bushel for her, and he didn't wait for her to go ahead of him.

He simply shouted, "Come along then!" he shouted, expecting her to follow his commands.

Maria brought herself to her feet, picked up the bushel, and followed in line with Joe's footsteps. Even though people said he was crazy, he was still a man, and she'd better do as she was instructed.

By the time the unlikely pair reached the cottage, Francesco was already at the Zinc Works, and Joe wasn't about to converse with Concetta. He knew better, for as much as young Italian women were leading a subservient life to the men of the family, the elder Italian women were a silent force to be reckoned with when it came to discussing their family.

"I'll speak with your father soon," uttered Joe, turning to continue down the hill on his morning journey.

Gruff and abrasive as Crazy Joe was, he had accompanied a weary Maria back to the safety of her home. He could've left her lying back there on that path without stopping to check on her welfare.

What had happened to me? Maria couldn't help but wonder.

All she could remember was feeling a bit dizzy, and the next thing she knew, Crazy Joe's dog was licking the sweat from her forehead.

Of course, Crazy Joe took little time in reporting to Francesco that his daughter was sleeping alongside the path instead of tending to her duties at home. This was an uncharacteristic situation for Maria, and given his concern over her pale complexion, it didn't take Francesco long to retain an appointment with a doctor for his only remaining daughter. Francesco concealed terrifying thoughts of what could be wrong with his precious daughter. Of course, he was certain that she was suffering from a deadly illness that would render him helpless all over again. For a man barely age fifty, he had seen his share of tragic loss. He understood that tragedy has no boundary, and there was nothing forbidding God from taking Maria, too, if He so chose.

Finally, the day had arrived when Maria would see the doctor. The waiting room was cold, damp, and uninviting. Maria noticed a crack along the floorboards erupting to the ceiling of the dismal, painted wall. She wanted so much to be somewhere else, anywhere else. If she could've crawled inside that crack like a spider, she would've. Francesco and Maria sat almost silent in their uncomfortable, thinly padded chairs while Doc Peck hummed loudly in the next room. Finally, the humming subsided. Doc Peck appeared in the room with the pair.

"Alright, Maria. Follow me, please," Doc instructed.

He led her to an even smaller room with a little wooden table that reminded Maria of the tables she had seen bodies displayed on for a wake.

"Let's have you step up onto this exam table and see what seems to be the trouble," said Doc Peck in a memorized line. He began to examine Maria by looking in her eyes, ears, mouth, and throat. Maria felt the coolness of his stethoscope on her skin as he listened to her heart.

"Her heart sounds fine, Francesco," reported Doc Peck. That was the response that Francesco was waiting for. He felt a release of emotion as if he were an Egyptian slave, suddenly relieved of the ponderous bag of sand he carried on his back. The words virtually brought Francesco to tears. Losing his dear Nicolena to a heart defect made the possibility of another child also having a defect very real to Francesco. He was so moved by the moment that he did not notice the concern on Doc Peck's face as he continued to examine Maria.

"Perhaps, Francesco, I would ask you to wait in the other room for a bit while I complete my examination?" requested the doctor.

"Oh yes, yes, of course," Francesco responded without a moment's concern. He stood to his feet and left the room, thanking God in his mind all the way to the quiet, barren waiting area.

"How old are you now, Maria?" began Doc.

"I just turned twenty," she quickly responded.

"You have a lot of responsibilities at home, do you not? What with your mother and family?" questioned Doc.

"We work together to do what is needed for our family," Maria stated.

"Do you have a boyfriend? Perhaps someone you spend private time with?" Doc's questions began to make Maria a bit uncomfortable.

"No, I don't have a boyfriend," Maria retorted.

"I don't think I have any extra time right now for that!" Maria joked.

Doc Peck just continued with his examination but was now quiet except for the occasional "uh-huh" as though he were making a mental list of groceries. All at once, Doc announced he had finished his exam.

"Is everything okay?" Maria asked.

"Let's bring your father back in to discuss our situation," ordered Doc.

"Please get dressed, Maria, and I will collect your father from the waiting room, then I will come for you."

Times being what they were, it was not appropriate for the doctor to discuss Maria's medical condition without her father present. In fact, Francesco would have received the diagnosis before Maria.

Francesco was still silently thanking God for giving this daughter a good heart when the doc stepped into the aging, starkly clad waiting area.

"Come with me, Francesco. Let's have a seat in my office," Doc requested to Francesco as he held the door open for the concerned father.

The two men sat down in the doctor's private office while Maria waited alone with only her thoughts in her tiny exam room. Her thoughts were filled with all the duties she would be late in completing today due to what turned out to be a lengthy appointment. She could hear the muffled sounds of voices speaking through the wall but was unable to distinguish the topic of discussion. Finally, the mumbling ceased, and a moment later, the door to Maria's exam room opened with a creak.

"Maria, please come with me," requested Doc Peck in a low, concerning tone. Maria began to feel even more apprehensive about what was about to take place.

Doc Peck slowly opened the old squeaky oak door to his office and gestured for Maria to enter. The room was small and barely able to handle all the confined scents that filled the air as they spilled out into the hallway, like so many seeds in a milk pod. The mix of isopropyl alcohol, fine tobacco, and soap entered Maria's nasal passages. She felt a bit dizzy and nauseated as her eyes met Francesco's. He was as emotional about his family as he was strong for them. Maria saw that his brown eyes were filled with tears, and he massaged his forehead as though his skin was too tight. Her father's eyes were fixed on the woven carpet that revealed a warn path, exposing the fact that Doc Peck only traveled one route to get to the chair behind his desk, where he now sat and began the conversation with Maria and Francesco.

"Maria, we know why you fainted on the trail last week. Do you know?" stated Doc in a tone of certainty.

The room was silent, and Maria could hear her heart beating inside of her chest. She must of course, be dying with all this obvious gloom. Maria wasn't dying. In fact, it was quite the opposite.

"Maria, when I asked you if you had a gentleman friend, you told me no. I have to dispute that statement even though I have never known you to lie," said the doctor.

"What do you mean?" Maria questioned. "I didn't lie to you, and I don't have a gentleman friend."

"Maria, you are going to have a baby. My guess would be late this winter," reported the doctor.

The knock-out power of those words, uttered so matter-of-factly by Doc Peck, momentarily robbed Maria of her breath. The stillness of the room was ringing loudly in Maria's ears, making her dizzy. It could've been the paleness of her face, the emptiness of her stare, or perhaps the reality of reaction falling down her cheek that summoned Francesco to her side. She felt the warmth of his gentle hug of defeat all around her. Strong, loving arms that wanted to absorb every challenging experience that lay ahead for her. Doc Peck excused himself from the room to allow the father and daughter a few minutes to process the reality of what was. There was no discussion, no questions, and no presentation of reason exchanged between the two. In fact, no words were spoken. They both remained arm in arm, sobbing together, one supporting the other, forming a bipod of strength, preventing neither one from collapsing. Those few moments spoke volumes of a lifetime of commitment in love between father and daughter.

Thirty minutes later, Doc returned.

"We have some matters that we need to discuss, my friends," offered a concerned Doc Peck.

Francesco allowed himself to open his eyes, which were now stinging and red from the weight of his tears.

"Let us see where God is guiding us," uttered Francesco to Maria as he put his arm on her shoulder.

"First of all, Maria, you must inform this child's father, as I'm sure your father will want to arrange a quick marriage," suggested the helpful doc. "After that has been done, you will come to see me as a patient every few weeks until you have the baby."

"There cannot be a marriage, Doc," said a reluctant Maria.

"Don't be silly, child. There must be a wedding now. No one expects you to shoulder this alone," retorted Doc Peck.

"Of course, there will be a marriage!" stated Francesco with bewilderment on his face. "I will not allow a man to take this liberty and not honor his duty."

"Oh, father, there can be only one person responsible for this, and he is already married," sobbed Maria.

Doc Peck and Francesco locked eyes in disbelief. "What do you mean, Maria?" asked the doc.

For the next hour, Maria sat completely still, arms folded across her chest, staring at some distant nothing, and disclosed the entire horrific event with Marcello. Prior to that moment, she had never uttered a word about it, hoping it could remain forever in that dreadful closet. She felt like she was living inside a dream, a nightmare that had no beginning or end. A suspended state of bizarre euphoria in sharing the facts of that terrible Saturday morning with her father and doctor.

"This will require more consideration, I do believe," proclaimed Doc.

"Yes, Maria, we will need time to put this all together and discuss how we move ahead with all this information," said Francesco angrily.

Maria wasn't sure to whom Francesco intended his anger, but she hoped it was not for her. As the shattered immigrants left the doctor's office, Maria again noted the crack along the floor that extended up the wall to the ceiling. This was such a metaphor now. Her life and the lives of her family were cracked forever. Could this ever be repaired, or was it destined to be a fracture from bottom to top?

Nineteen

The next few days moved like the molten lava of Vesuvius—slow and destructive. Times being what they were, it was quickly decided that Maria, being a woman, in all probability, was lying about the encounter with Marcello. She surely seduced the unsuspecting older man, and he merely gave in to his manly needs. Even though Maria's parents knew that her lips only spoke truth, they accepted the reality she would not be believed and must bear the responsibility of guilt. Arrangements were contemplated and prayed on. The priest at their parish caught wind of the south side gossip and quickly presented at the humble home of Francesco and Concetta.

Father O'Shea was a kindhearted soul who truly meant well. At Masses, Maria was always preoccupied with studying his long, pale fingers as he waved them through the air to accentuate the word of God. They were like spider legs, wisping through the air. His oversized knuckles seemed to belong on another's hand. He was over six feet tall and rail-thin. His curly red hair toppled over his forehead, and those vibrant, mischievous blue eyes revealed his Irish roots. His large and inviting smile was his best problem-solver and peacemaker. Through that smile, he spoke with a strong brogue the word of an all-welcoming, nonjudgmental, and all-forgiving God. He was a well-respected man in the Catholic community.

"Come in, Father," offered Francesco as he held the door as wide as it would open.

"Thank you, Francesco," replied Father.

Francesco invited Father O'Shea to make himself comfortable in their home. Father O'Shea tugged at the front of his pants pockets, pulling them upward to accommodate a comfortable sitting position. This was an indication to Francesco that Father intended to sit awhile. Maria was in the summer kitchen where she was planning the evening meal. Although Francesco suspected Father O'Shea was there to discuss Maria, he didn't want to appear presumptuous.

"What welcome gesture brings you to our home today, Father?" questioned Francesco as he motioned to Maria to bring Father a cup of coffee.

"It has come to my attention that you may need my assistance. I'm referring to your most recent dilemma with Maria," stated Father O'Shea.

Maria could not help but overhear as the water in the coffee pot issued a hissing sound, signaling its preparedness. The unmistakable sound brought her thoughts back to the reality that she would have to interact with Father O'Shea. Maria had known Father for several years and enjoyed his friendship. Her embarrassment and shame now took over, and her hands trembled as she poured the coffee into a small cup. She then proceeded to offer the cup to Father O'Shea. His long, thin fingers, which had been draped over his thighs like a blanket, gratefully reached out to accept the cup. He then promptly set it down on the small, worn side table, an indication of more pressing matters than sipping coffee.

"Maria, please join us here for a moment, won't you?" Father invited.

Francesco gestured for Maria to sit. As Maria allowed her knees to bend, she became inherently aware of the weight of her body. When she made contact with the chair, she could feel herself dissolve into its cushion. The burden of secrecy was no longer hers to carry, for if Father O'Shea knew, all the south side knew. As tragic as it was that her secret was no longer hers, Maria felt a sense of great relief. As if talking out loud about it would take away any guilt she possessed. She imagined Mrs. Romano's tale of the events and her animated details. Maria's relief at the release of the secret was swift and fleeting as Father spoke his next words.

"There is a home I know of in Milwaukee that will accept Maria and assist her with needs as they arise." I have already made contact with the Sister in charge, and she is expecting Maria on Saturday," stated Father O'Shea in a matter-of-fact tone.

Panic flooded over Maria like a giant tsunami wave. It engulfed her entire body, and for a few seconds she believed she had misheard Father. Her mind raced from one thought to another as tears began streaming down both tanned cheeks.

"Now, Maria, this is what's best for everyone. Your parents cannot endure the scrutiny that will no doubt be present daily. You will need care as you prepare to deliver a baby. The nuns will teach you how to take care of yourself and how to pray until this situation passes. I've also arranged for a daily helper for Concetta while Maria is away," said Father as his spiny fingers interlocked with each other.

The coldness and detachment of his words were like the sharp edge of an icicle hanging off the eave on a cold winter day. The sting of their finality hurt like the smokehouse door when you allowed it to slam closed before getting your heels out of its path.

What did he mean … until this situation passes? thought Maria. Her dark eyes darted to Francesco for the answer.

The loss of dear Nicolena, now his beloved daughter Maria, all but banished from their sweet little town. Had Francesco written his own story of coming to America, none of these events would have happened. Now he surrenders his strength to Father O'Shea and agrees that Maria will travel to an abbey in Milwaukee to deliver her baby.

Despite Maria's begging to stay in the little stone cottage, Father O'Shea's recommendation would win out. Francesco and Concetta stood wounded deeply at their little wooden door as they kissed their only living daughter farewell on the morning of September 10, 1932. It was an ominous day with dense fog clinging to the hill. *The weather is fitting*, thought Maria, given the weight of her mind. What would become of her and her unborn child? How would she survive in a strange, new place not knowing a single soul?

Concetta stood weakly as she hugged her daughter tight. How the circle of life had spun; not so long ago, she had been the traveler receiving the loving hug of her own mother as she embarked on an unknown journey. Now she truly felt the spirit of her mother, who had been so brave all those years before. What strength it must've taken for Concetta's mother to let go. But this was different. Concetta wanted to go, but Maria did not. Father O'Shea saw the protective sparkle in Concetta's eyes and responded quickly.

"Now, now. She will be fine," Father stated as he waved his hand in a most dismissive manner.

How would he know? Maria thought to herself.

Maria began to realize that she had never been too fond of Father O'Shea, and now she could not look at him. Who was this man to tear her away from her family, which she needed now more than ever? How could he possibly understand?

Father O'Shea's Model T noisily made its way down the hill, hitting every bump in the road as she waved, tears streaming down her face. As Maria's body swiveled around in the uncomfortable seat, her eyes focused on the road. She would leave her happiness at the bottom of the hill fully intending to pick it back up when she returned. As Father gave the car more speed, Maria gave herself permission to close the door to the outside world. She placed herself inside a room in her head, along with all her cherished thoughts and her family. As if covering all the furniture in a room that wouldn't be used in a while, Maria looked to the future only. Perhaps she knew of what lay ahead. Perhaps she knew there would be no room to harbor anything but strength for getting through each day at the abbey.

Concetta, too, watched as the black automobile turned the bend at the bottom of the hill. It was an all too familiar memory of her own experience with separation, only this time she was painfully aware of the uncertainties. What would become of their beautiful daughter and her unborn child? How long would Maria be away? Would she ever return? Why had any of this even happened?

As if sensing Concetta's silent concerns, Francesco hugged his wife strongly. "God will protect Maria, my darling. This I am sure of." Then he slowly turned her aging body and helped her to a chair. Maria had done so much. Life in the stone house would be much different for Francesco and Concetta now.

Twenty

The Milwaukee area had several institutions of what Father O'Shea called "opportunities for assistance in a time of need." He spoke to Maria about the services she would be granted as they continued the lengthy journey to Milwaukee. He pointed out to her that she was one of the fortunate ones to have been chosen for admission to such a wholesome, caring facility. It wasn't that Father O'Shea was lying; he really believed in the integrity of the organization. Maria became hopeful that her experience would be a nonjudgmental and helpful environment as the car slowed into the parking area of a large brick building.

The room was dimly lit, and it held a multitude of religious statues. Maria felt as if the eyes of each statue were filled with shame focused directly on her. It was an uneasy judgment, and it felt uncomfortable. The aged room was impeccably clean except for a small smudge in the far corner of the floor. The rug beneath her well-worn shoes had seen better days, but the rug and the shoes complemented each other and seemed to acknowledge their tired journey through time. Three wooden, unwelcoming chairs lined the opposite wall. Maria wondered how many other young women had found themselves warming those uncomfortable seats over the years. Where were those women now, and what had their experience been? A large bookcase covered one wall. There were books about faith, about child rearing, and about avoiding sin. Maria turned her head from the bookshelf as if to strike it from her mind. She closed her eyes, dropped her head into her hands, and supported it with her forearms and upper legs to avoid the stares of the statues. So far, there didn't seem to be anything to mirror the facility Father O'Shea described to her during the drive to Milwaukee. She had been told to wait in this dismal room while Father O'Shea met with the Reverend Mother, but she didn't care to learn any more details of the room. *What must they be discussing that is taking so long?* Maria thought.

As if her wish was a command, the heavy door of the Reverend Mother's office creaked open. Father O'Shea exited the office, and the door closed behind him.

"You will be fine now, Maria," he said as he touched her shoulder. "The Reverend Mother will see to that. Now, you're to wait here just a bit longer, and she will greet you. However, I must be on my way. God Bless you, my child. I'll pray for you," said Father O'Shea.

Just like that, he was gone, and Maria was left alone with the staring statues. She sat back down on the uncomfortable wooden chair scantly padded in a paisley print, now torturous to sit on. Perhaps its level of comfort was just a precursor of the weeks to come at this retreat for unwed mothers.

Sister Mary's shoelaces were the first thing about her that Maria's eyes focused on as the elderly nun stepped through the doorway and into the waiting area. They were laced up tight, perfectly tied, and her heels made a sharp clicking sound when they struck the floor. Despite the intimidating shoes, Sister Mary wore a kind smile and caring eyes. She held out her arms to Maria in a hug-like gesture of welcome.

"Hello, Maria. Welcome to our home," she said in a soft and reverent voice.

"Thank you, Sister," replied Maria respectfully as she stood to receive the gesture.

Sister Mary then proceeded to lead Maria on a tour of the facility, complete with introductions to the other nuns who passed by as they made their way through the hallways. Maria felt so ashamed, as if each nun was staring in the same disappointed way the statues of the waiting area were. To Maria, everyone possessed the same pathetic glance toward her, and her guilt was profound.

When Sister Mary and Maria reached what was to be Maria's room, Sister Mary excused herself to allow Maria some time to get to know her surroundings. Sister Mary informed Maria of mealtimes and that Sister Catherine would be her guardian and counsel during her stay.

"You will meet Sister Catherine shortly," Sister Mary stated as she closed the heavy door behind her.

Maria sat on the bed. All alone in a strange city, with strange people. She thought about her parents and how she hated being away from them. Still, surely this was the best way to handle her situation as it would be better for all, or that's what everyone said anyway.

When the knock came at the door, Maria stood.

"Come in," she reluctantly spouted.

The door opened with a small creak, and another pair of pointed black shoes stepped into the room. Although the same type of shoe, there was little resemblance with Sister Mary's. These shoes were haphazardly tied, and the smooth part of the leather was streaked with scuffs. The loops were dreadfully uneven, allowing part of her stocking to peek through the tongue of the shoe. They also did not make the sharp clicking sound on the flooring; they were virtually silent as they struck the floor. These were the shoes of a working nun, a busy nun, and a purposeful nun with much more important tasks than perfecting her laces.

"Maria, I am Sister Catherine. You may call me Sister or Sister Catherine," she proclaimed rather sternly.

Sister Catherine proceeded to outline the structure of life in the home and what the expectations were of Maria. Maria was free to roam about the home and gardens but could not leave the property. Mealtimes were strictly enforced, and if you missed the mealtime, you did not eat. Each young lady was required to attend studies at the proper times, and any "shenanigans," as Sister Catherine called it, would not be tolerated. Maria had absolutely no idea what shenanigans were, but from the tone of Sister's voice, it wasn't something good. After a short and informational meeting, Sister Catherine's admission was complete.

"I'll leave you to reflection now," dismissed Sister Catherine as she gestured toward a distressed wooden rocking chair in the corner. It was a companion to the bed, nightstand, and a picture of the Virgin Mary on the wall. A simple room with simple necessities. Maria placed her small suitcase on the bed as the door closed behind the scuffed shoes. She looked over at the lovely painting of the Virgin Mary. *How fitting*, she thought. Another pair of eyes to reveal her misery, but these eyes somehow seemed softer, more forgiving, and more soothing to Maria.

As she unpacked her meager belongings, tears of the unknown rolled down her lovely olive-colored cheeks. How alone she felt and how very far from home she seemed to be—farther than she had ever been. Oh, how she missed her mother and father, the little stone cottage, and all the people in her life. What must they think of her? Could she ever return home? Why was banishment the only option for a young woman? What had she done wrong to deserve this segregation?

That first night in the Milwaukee home for girls was one of the longest of Maria's life. There was no visible moon that dark September night, signaling to Maria that dark days could be ahead. The distant hallway sounds were infrequent and swift when they occurred. Nighttime was quiet time, and everyone adhered to the rules. When morning came, the sun did indeed rise, much to Maria's surprise, and the world moved forward.

The fall leaves and scents comforted Maria as she settled into daily life in the house. She met other young women who also had become pregnant through different circumstances, some more appalling than Maria's case. She enjoyed their friendship and comradery, but her heart remained heavy. The "studies" that Sister Mary had referred to upon admission to the home were actually spiritual retreats and self-reflection. To Maria and most of the other girls, these classes seemed like daily punishment and a reminder of their "sinful" lifestyles.

The details and events of Maria's months in the girls' home, or what the time would refer to as an unwed mother's home, were eventful and telling. Seeds for another day's planting.

By the time the frigid February temps rolled around, Maria was tired of watching the featherlike snowfall, tired of its blanketed sparkling beauty on the perfectly manicured lawn of the home, and tired of feeling hopeless. She missed her parents terribly, and their letters were simply not enough to replace their warm hugs and joyous laughter. Oh, how she missed family mealtime, working side by side with her mother, and their little stone cottage on the hill. She even missed Mrs. Romano and her gossiping, a thought that made Maria smile.

Twenty-One

It was February 20 and eleven degrees below zero. It seemed that the world would never be warm again. Everything would remain frozen, dismal, and cold forever. Maria attended her study time in the great hall as required, but this day was different. Maria felt more restless and uncomfortable than she had throughout the entire pregnancy. She couldn't get into a comfortable position. Sister Agnes, who presided over the study, noticed Maria fidgeting in her seat.

"Maria, are you alright?" she asked.

Sister Agnes was a very kindhearted soul. Maria loved her and enjoyed spending time in her presence. She was always uplifting and positive, even when it was difficult. She gave hugs and made each girl aware of her importance to God as well as to others. She just had a special way of making things seem alright, even when they weren't.

"I'm okay, Sister," Maria replied.

"Please come to my desk, Maria," Sister Agnes requested as she motioned forward with her hand.

"Now tell me, my dear, how do you feel?" Sister Agnes asked as Maria reached her.

"Well, my lower back is aching today, and I'm just fidgety."

"Maria, my dear, I want you to go back to your room now. Someone will be down to speak to you shortly. Just rest until then," instructed Sister Agnes.

Maria did as she was told but turned back instinctively to gaze once more at Sister Agnes's lovely face and feel the genuine concern it was emanating.

As the hours passed, Maria's back pain progressed into the labor of childbirth. Sister Catherine was also a nurse, and she would stay close to Maria until delivery. *Oh please*, Maria thought, *anyone but Sister Catherine*. Maria wasn't sure what had happened to Sister Catherine's compassion. Perhaps it had been swallowed up by those heavy, long black robes. Or maybe it was squeezed out through her tight habit. Maria wasn't sure how or where the compassion had disappeared, but she was certain it was not present in Sister Catherine's heart.

Maria's friends, also young soon-to-be mothers, were not allowed to visit her while in labor. The Sisters determined that it was in the best interest of the function of the home if the girls were kept separate from the group while laboring. So, Maria lay quietly on her bed with Sister Catherine at her side, all the while reading scripture aloud. With each contraction, Sister Catherine merely looked over her shiny wire-rimmed glasses and say, "Just keep breathing!" Then her empty, dark eyes would return to the Bible passage she was reading. Maria couldn't have felt more alone than if she were the last fall leaf clinging to a cold branch on a single tree at the end of a quiet road during a fall windstorm.

Suddenly, there came a knock at Maria's door. Sister Catherine's scripture reading finally subsided while she rose to answer the door. Maria watched her as she stood next to the door, her thin, frail hand on the doorknob, the back of her head moving in rhythm with her words to whoever was on the other side of the door. Sister Catherine's voice was low at first, and then it rose a few decibels as her head seemed to gesture her disagreement. All at once, her frail hand swung open the door, and she allowed the visitor access to the room. It was Sister Agnes. She immediately approached Maria and touched her hand.

"How are you doing, my child?" she inquired.

"I am scared, and the pain is quite intense."

"I know you are scared, but God is with you, and I will be with you through the night, my dear," Sister Agnes whispered as her eyes gave the soft glow of support and strength. She then turned toward Sister Catherine and gave a smile.

Sister Catherine once again looked over her glasses and then immediately resumed her dictation of the Bible. The rhythmic sounds of Sister Catherine's reading and the soft, warm touch of Sister Agnes's hand on Maria's brow allowed her to sleep for a bit. Maria felt truly cared for and loved for the first time in months.

The light of day was just beginning to creep in through the window curtain when a violent pain in Maria's abdomen awakened her. It was morning, and the contractions were now more intense, longer, and more frequent. Both Sister Catherine and Sister Agnes looked as fatigued as Maria felt but remained close to her now.

"We have called the doctor, Maria. He will be coming in shortly," advised Sister Agnes while Sister Catherine prepared things along the wall of Maria's room. For an instant, Maria wondered what Sister Catherine was doing, but then a contraction began, and Maria no longer cared what Sister Catherine was doing just as long as her recitation of biblical readings had stopped!

The doctor arrived by the time the room was fully lit by the winter sun. Maria thought it was probably mid-morning. Dr. Kelly had white hair and a scant mustache that twitched when he spoke. He said very little and seemed to be somewhat inconvenienced by being there. Sister Agnes continued to give Maria her full support and kind attention.

At 11:43 a.m., February 21, 1933, a newborn baby girl loudly acknowledged her arrival into the world. She was the most beautiful child Maria had ever seen. Even Sister Catherine could not deny how enchanting this little lady was. She had black hair and long fingers that formed a petite fist. Her tiny dark eyes and olive-colored skin revealed her attachment to the past, but her cry of existence proclaimed her position in the future.

It would be years later before Maria fully understood the gravity of that moment. For now, the business of motherhood and learning how to care for a child consumed her. Maria certainly knew how to care for another, but this would be different somehow. This little cherub would grow up without the stigma of immigrant status. This little girl was an American, despite her dark skin. Not an outsider and not the child of an outsider, but a true American. For this, Maria was happy as she began to feel a little less fuzzy from the ether. Maria could barely make out the outline of Sister Agnes leaning over the bed speaking. Maria tried hard to focus on her lovely voice.

"How are you doing, Maria?" Sister Agnes quietly whispered. "You don't have to talk now. You just rest. Your little girl is doing fine, and we will take good care of her."

Maria nodded her head in agreement. Her eyelids refused to unmask her pupils, and much of the moment was unclear. What was clear to Maria was that Sister Agnes had spent many hours at her side in support of her efforts. This fact would always hold a safe corner in Maria's memory closet. No other stranger had ever shown her such compassion.

The days following the birth of Maria's baby went quickly. This was a home for unwed mothers-to-be, not an apartment house. One week after giving birth to her perfect little daughter, Sister Agnes and Sister Catherine appeared in Maria's room.

"Maria, you have to make your decision today," stated Sister Catherine.

"What decision?" questioned Maria as Sister Agnes sat beside her on the bed.

"Your baby needs to be in another part of our house with the other infants who will be adopted," Sister Catherine coldly stated.

"What are you talking about? protested Maria. "My baby will not be adopted. She will go home with me to live with my family," she retorted.

"Now, Maria, you are in no position to raise a child. Your family is a poor immigrant family that has trouble making ends meet already. Why not give this child the chance to have more than you have? Give her a life with opportunity and promise. What can you offer her? We have many families waiting to adopt a perfect child such as this," explained Sister Catherine as Sister Agnes took Maria's hand in hers.

It was then Maria saw the emptiness in Sister Catherine's eyes. There was no warmth or love for others, just emptiness and bone-chilling cold. How could she say these words so matter-of-fact and have no emotion? Maria just stared straight ahead in disbelief. Never at any time did she ever consider not taking this child home with her. Where did this idea come from? She needed to speak with her father and mother about what was happening.

Sister Catherine folded her arms and motioned to Sister Agnes to leave the room.

"We will proceed as planned, Sister," instructed Sister Catherine.

"Perhaps we should give the child a little more time to think and discuss this with her priest when he comes to collect her?" recommended Sister Agnes.

"Nonsense. These girls don't have the capacity to raise a child. There are so many capable couples in this city who are looking for newborns to welcome into their families, to love and cherish, and offer a positive future. We must assist in the placement of these dark children. That is difficult enough due to their skin. It is God's will, my Sister," boldly stated Sister Catherine as she smugly clicked the heels of her shoes down the tile-floored hallway. Maria became terrified that these women would keep her beautiful baby and send her home.

Maria was overjoyed to see the face of Father O'Shea as he quietly entered her small room later that afternoon.

"Oh, Father, I'm so happy to see you!" Maria shouted as she hugged him. She couldn't help feeling overwhelmed at the prospect of returning to her little stone cottage on the hill. She'd missed her parents, family, and hometown.

"Yes, yes, Maria. I'm happy to see you too," Father said, waving both hands as if fanning a fire.

"I've brought along your father as well. He insisted. He is waiting to greet you outside," said the priest.

Maria grabbed the handle of her small suitcase and began to head toward the door of her room.

"Please, Maria, just sit down for a moment," requested Father O'Shea.

Maria continued to stand, fingers gripping tightly on the handle of the small, tattered case. These many months of what she viewed as captivity had given Maria strength beyond measure. She wasn't the same young girl Father O'Shea had scooped up and swept away as if to hide a terrible secret that could never be told. It wasn't she who should have run away and hid. There was more to her than that, and now she knew it.

Twenty-Two

"Father O'Shea," Maria began, "I am ready to return to my home with my daughter. I am grateful for your guidance and assistance in getting me to this moment. However, today my daughter and I will be leaving here, never to return. All I would ask of you is a ride home and your continued prayers," Maria finished as her eyes never wavered from Father O'Shea's. Maria had no time to entertain his recommendations, suggestions, or guidance. The past few months had been difficult, but Maria had learned and grown. She was now sure of herself and would put her faith in who she was and who she could be. She had grown into a wiser, more informed, braver young woman, much like her mother had been.

There was a brief pause, then Father O'Shea rose to his feet. He put one hand on Maria's left shoulder and looked into her eyes. He must've known there was nothing left to be said. The decision, if there had been one, was already made. He walked slowly toward the door and opened it. It creaked loudly as it swung from its hinges, seemingly in an effort to release the pain of the last few months. At last, bright sunshine spilled its way across Maria's feet. There in the doorway reflecting the bright sunshine was Sister Agnes. She held a tiny miracle wearing a lace bonnet wrapped in a warm blanket. Sister Agnes advanced into the room and went directly to Maria.

"Here is your miracle, Maria." Sister Agnes gently laid the beautiful dark-eyed baby in her mother's arms. "May God's love surround her and you always," said Sister Agnes to Maria as she stroked her hair.

Maria took a moment to take one last look at the tiny room with a single bed and one tattered dresser that had been her home for the last several months. She felt the heaviness of the air, filled with painful memories. Even though she was so grateful to be leaving it behind, she felt a little bit of her innocence reflecting off the walls. She lifted her free hand to touch the doorway, which felt warm with memories that must not cross the threshold. For just a moment, the forward-moving rotation of the earth paused, and then, like a wave erasing footprints in the sand, Maria allowed herself to pass through the door, leaving it all behind.

As Maria stepped outside the home for girls, she immediately saw the gentle eyes of her father. She ran to him, embracing him with all that she was. How wonderful it felt to be reunited with her dear father. Maria took a step back to unveil the beauty wrapped with the lovely pink blanket.

"She is certainly a beautiful child, my sweet," proclaimed Francesco.

"Oh, Papa, they wanted me to give her away to the nuns! I could never do that!" shouted Maria.

"Come, my dear, we will all return home together this day," replied Francesco.

The ride home from Milwaukee was uneventful for Maria. Father O'Shea and her papa had several conversations during the trip, but Maria was mesmerized by the little lady in the blanket. She felt very blessed.

Once back home in the little stone cottage on the hill, life had somewhat returned to normal—however, a new normal for Maria. Many of the south side had plenty of time to discuss Maria in her absence. There were a lot of scorns, looks of discontent, and even hurtful words slung Maria's way. Even though these situations were painful and troublesome to Maria, she rose above them. She was focused on her mother, father, and baby girl, whom she had named Mary.

As Mary grew, life remained a challenge for the resilient immigrant family. Maria continued caring for her aging mother and father and providing guidance and teachings to Mary. Francesco grew old, and the beautiful olive skin of Concetta became wrinkled and careworn. Time has no mercy and would not wait for their dreams. Francesco had spent the months of Maria's absence learning that nothing was more important than his family, critics be damned. He had faced adversity before; that's all he'd ever known. Maria and Mary were the joy of his life, and he would spend the rest of it showing them just how much he loved them. Nothing gave him a wider smile than little Mary playing in the yard under the big oak tree where the sweet singing of the wren could be heard loudly. Francesco had no doubt this wren was a descendant of that first wren that led Francesco to the little house. Their families had evolved together to become a part of this land.

Concetta was as much a part of the household as she'd always been, just in a much quieter way. Her silky silver hair was always neatly rolled up in a bun nestled against the back of her head. Maria would help with this chore as Concetta no longer possessed the dexterity to manipulate it herself. Her days were spent visiting and counseling the younger Italian ladies, many of whom would visit daily. Concetta's beauty never left her presence; it was true, lasting, and eternal. Her body was slowing, but her mind was as wise as any sage. They had endured life and lived it to this point. What more could one ask? They felt blessed to be surrounded by family, and they were happy. That was enough.

Twenty-Three

That December morning began like every other winter morning in the little stone cottage on the hill. Francesco was adding a log to the stove for Maria to begin an early breakfast. The sun turned the sparkling snow a peculiar shade of blue, and the barren trees appeared particularly black and ominous that day. Winter made for extra work and longer days encased by darkness. The scent of hickory wood slowly burning, accompanied by the smoked pork scent of the bacon Maria was slicing, made the early dawn hours an experience in home comforts, despite the hard work. Sundays were always a busy morning for Maria. She needed to prepare the breakfast, help Concetta dress for the day, and assist little Mary as needed while keeping mindful of Mass start time. Still, the morning events passed in perfect precision due to Maria's planning and repetitive practice. It wasn't until after Mass that the little immigrant family learned of the terrible evil that shook the land that day.

Not many of the small congregation in attendance that December day knew where Hawaii was, but the gravity of comprehending the cruel attack on Pearl Harbor brought forth a shadow of sorrow to the people. The sorrow and sadness, however, could not have prepared the small town for what lay ahead. No one anticipated or could possibly be prepared for the sacrifice that would soon follow.

Francesco stooped over to tune the dial on the secondhand radio—the same radio Mr. Townsley had refurbished. Mr. Townsley always told Maria she needed to be what he termed "in touch with the world." On this day, Maria wished that perhaps the world could be tuned out. Still, the importance of the moment was unparalleled. The news was devastating. So many men killed, so many unaccounted for, and so very many injured. The declaration of war by the president came across the airwaves like a giant counterweight, one that would pull everyone from happiness and contentment.

Before long, there were truckloads of men heading to the local recruiting station to sign up for the service. Those who didn't volunteer could expect official correspondence from the U.S. government declaring that each male household member aged eighteen to forty-five report to a specific recruiting station for their selective service. It seemed unreal to think of but just one year prior, as if by some cruel means of foretelling the future, men of a particular age were required to register. No time was lost in the building of a large fighting force.

The south side of town was hit hard, as was every small community. Hadn't the immigrants sacrificed enough? They gambled everything to come to a new land, adopt its policies, and become Americans. They had left their families and everything they ever knew to make this better life possible. Now the very land they were striving so hard to become a part of wanted their sons in trade. Each Italian household that had sons now grew quiet and solemn. Prayers were taken to a whole new level. Many mothers spent countless hours in meditative prayer, sometimes alone and sometimes as a group. Concetta and Francesco struggled with the idea of three of their sons being sent to the recruiting center. By the grace of God, only one son was sent to the European theatre. For this, Francesco was thankful, but even one son was too great a price to pay.

However, this immigrant family had resilience and stamina. They would pray for the strength and faith that their son would come back to them. So many families had several sons serving in the very homelands their immigrant parents had long ago left behind. One of Maria's favorite Italian families had five sons serving in Europe. As always, immigrants did whatever it took to be successful and move forward in their new lives. This challenge, while different, was indeed just another challenge. In private, Francesco and Concetta would

112

THAT WAS ENOUGH

sob and question how this could be possible, but their strong bravery and faith would sustain their hearts. Perhaps the being that was WWII was unaware of the caliber of people who would be tested. Perhaps the measure of their strength and determination was underestimated. This group of people had been tested and challenged every day of their lives. They simply knew no other way of living but that of continued trials of which you couldn't give up on.

Trials and challenges would indeed continue for the immigrant families, the other families in the community, as well as the entire country. Food rations were implemented to facilitate the war effort, and citizens were glad to do their part in support. The south side was not unique in their quiet day-to-day existence. Even joyous events and shared chores now seemed lacking in fulfillment, all due to the overshadowing of this terrible war and the absence of so many sons, husbands, fathers, and friends. Every Thursday outside the public library door a list typed on a 1915 Underwood typewriter appeared, revealing the names of the men who would not be coming home—those who had believed in something larger than themselves so strongly that they surrendered their lives for it. Maria would pass by on Mondays and pause to read each name. Most on the list she knew personally and felt a sense of sorrow for each one. She made a conscious effort to pray for their families and the souls of who these men were or would've been. Concetta was also very much aware of the dangers her son now faced. Maria tried valiantly to keep her calm about the war, but there was no dismissing her worries. Oh, how they prayed that their son and brother's name would never be listed on this dreaded page.

When the war finally ended, Maria's brother would return to his beloved small town. He was fortunate, unlike many immigrant sons who perished in WWII. It was the mid-1940s, and America was, once again, joyful and determined. The shade of darkness had finally lifted, and people could smile again. Concetta and Francesco maintained the glimmer in their eyes, but their bodies had grown old. The stress of time had demanded its wage. Francesco and Concetta had lived a life like no other. They felt content with the life they had built and insisted that the only thing they would've done differently would've been to save Nicolena from an inevitable death somehow. Of course, at the time, they all knew it was not a possibility. Their journey of life had been difficult and yet fulfilling. They had successfully settled into a new land for their children and their children's children to enjoy. They now grew tired upon entering the quiet time of life.

Twenty-Four

When Francesco died, his body was reverently displayed in the family living area of the little stone cottage. Concetta was assisted to the edge of the coffin by two of her sons. She gazed at this gentle, loving man as he lay there so peacefully. She reached up with her bent fingers, now reshaped by arthritis, and grasped his hand. She spoke softly, sweetly, and from the heart.

In Italian, she whispered, "Go be with God, for you have journeyed the good journey. You have brought us through this life with all that you are. Rest well, my husband, and take care of our sweet Nicolena until I can join you in heaven." So much of life had been a promise of faith, a guarantee that something better would be just around the corner. Concetta had hoped that for Francesco, his journey had been fulfilling.

For three days and nights Francesco lay in the living room of the stone cottage. On the fourth day, the sun rose, and the funeral wagon sat outside. Maria was up with the sun to prepare the food, assisted by many other Italian women. Concetta and each of their children gave their final goodbyes to Francesco as the funeral director slid the top onto the coffin. Now more of a teen, Little Mary ran to the side of the wooden planked board to sneak one last peek at her grandfather. The funeral director obliged her wishes and allowed her the final opportunity of attempting to memorize each line of his tired face. The tears cried that day were genuine tears of love for a man who gave all he was and asked for nothing in return. Even Mr. Townsley wept openly at the gravesite prayer service for the loss of such a dear friend. Perhaps it was he, Mr. Townsley, who first noticed her.

She stood in the back of the cemetery near the old, tattered, broken fence. No one remembered for sure who noticed her first. As the priest concluded his final remarks and each family member stood silent, Mr. Townsley approached the aging woman. As he prepared to offer his assistance so that she may come closer and join the group, the woman shied away. She pulled her dark scarf a little closer to her mouth. Her tawny skin and glistening dark eyes gave away her attempts to conceal that she was indeed Italian.

"Please, come forward and join us," Mr. Townsley welcomed with an outstretched arm and open hand.

The woman glanced backward to a waiting car and responded, "I'm sorry. I cannot."

"Alright, my sympathies to you, ma'am," Mr. Townsley quietly said as he retreated.

Mr. Townsley was an interesting fellow and could cure anyone's curiosity about the town. Of course, that made him the most curious person of all! He simply could not resist knowing who was in the strange auto and what in the world was going on. He knew everyone in the area and had no idea who this woman was.

As the small crowd dispersed from the garden of forgotten stones, Mr. Townsley approached the dark auto, which was forced to wait patiently until others departed. Walking ever closer, each step of his foot sunk ever so slightly into the damp, soft earth. Soon he could easily read the license plate, which revealed the car was from the state of Illinois. One occupant sat behind the wheel wearing a finely tailored brimmed hat. Mr. Townsley tapped on the car window, and the gentleman slowly rolled it down.

"You've come a long way today. Please be our guest at the home of our great friend who has now gone to his eternal rest," solemnly requested Mr. Townsley.

"Grazie," replied the driver. "I will consult with the senora. Indeed, it has been a long journey, but I am just the driver."

As he finished speaking, the cloaked woman opened the passenger back door and gently sat down. Her stature was small, and her movements were elegant. Her black dress was perfectly fitted, and the black scarf was silken as it reflected the sun's rays in its movement from her head to her lap. Her dark eyes then slowly lifted to meet Mr. Townsley's. He could see her cheeks were moist with the salty tears she must've shed for Francesco. She used her gloved hand to wipe them aside.

"How may we help you, sir?" she whispered in a faint voice.

"My name is Mr. Townsley, and I was explaining to your man here that you certainly have traveled a long way and must be hungry. I've known Francesco since he came to Mineral Point, and he would expect me to extend a hand of hospitality to those paying their respects to him and his family at this most difficult time."

"I'm so sorry, Mr. Townsley," the woman began without giving her name, "Francesco was a proud and gracious man; you are correct. But I would not be welcome in Concetta's home," she stated without question.

"Nonsense! I've never heard of anyone not welcome in Concetta's home!" insisted Mr. Townsley. He had known this to be the absolute truth. "You obviously have never met Concetta!" he challenged.

"To correct you, kind sir, she has never met me, but I have encountered her. I was present many years ago when she and Francesco were traveling through Chicago. At the time, my two daughters and I lived with Francesco's sister. Francesco and Concetta were on their journey to a new life and a new zinc operation here in Mineral Point. There was no need for Concetta and me to be introduced as she chose to make the journey north with Francesco instead of remaining in Chicago," the woman reported as if reliving the experience.

"Well, that is of no matter," started Mr. Townsley. "Surely you'd like to extend your thoughts to a dear woman who has lost her husband?"

This seemed to stir the woman's emotions away from her grieving and give them a sharper direction.

"I know all too well the feelings of the loss of a husband, sir. I, too, through circumstance of life, have lived many years without a husband."

Mr. Townsley could now sense the tenseness of her words in the air and was sorry he had stirred such an emotion to the surface. It was not in his nature to antagonize anyone, but clearly, he had done so. Before he could muster the words to apologize, she continued.

"I came to this country with my husband. It was a terrible journey. Many people died, and their bodies were just left in holding areas like stacked bags of potatoes. The illness and sickness on the ship was a sight I could not ever erase from my mind. When my husband left, I mourned for him, I mourned for my home in Italy, but I could not face the journey again aboard a ship to return to my home. The trauma of immigrating to America left me in a constant state of fear, which has been my lifelong companion. My husband left to find better work in a far away, remote area. I allowed my fears to make my decisions all my life. I stayed behind in Chicago with my young daughters because it felt safe. There were many people to help us and care for us. The city was growing, and there were opportunities for my children there. You see, kind sir, I loved my daughters more than I feared being without a husband," the mystery woman delivered.

"I'm so sorry. I didn't mean to cause you any trouble, ma'am," Mr. Townsley conveyed with sincerity.

"It is not your fault," she continued with a softened edge as she wiped her cheek again with the finger of those expensive gloves. "Only with age do we spend time in regret."

"I did not know Francesco had a sister in America," Mr. Townsley began, hoping to lighten the conversation.

This statement hung in the air for what seemed like several minutes before the beautiful, dark woman responded. It was as if each word was unlocking a door to the past she had kept closed and secret for decades. She sat up straight in the back seat, smoothed her skirt, and carefully folded her handkerchief in her lap as she began speaking.

"I grew up in Italy with Vittoria. We used to dance with the sunshine among the lemon trees," she remembered as her eyes fixed on an unknown point and her lips turned upward in a smile. "We were friends long before Francesco and I became friends. We grew up together in a world of perpetual love and happiness. I can still see Vittoria in all her commanding beauty as she stood next to me on the day I became her sister," the woman said as she paused to enjoy the memory.

Her eyes blinked, and she was back in the moment. Mr. Townsley stood mute as he couldn't process her memory quickly enough. His bewilderment created the look of understandable confusion on his aging face. The woman reached out with her tiny, gloved hand and placed it over the back of Mr.

118   THAT WAS ENOUGH

Townsley's hand which was resting on the top of the car door as she began.

"I can see that you, too, loved Francesco, so with you, and you alone, I will share these memories, and then I will return to Chicago to live out the rest of my days. My dear Vittoria left us three years ago on Mother's Day. I loved her no less than any sister. I came to America with her and my husband. My husband was her brother," she paused to glance up at Mr. Townsley.

"Yes, dear sir, as the look on your face exposes, that brother was Francesco, and I his wife. We have two lovely daughters together who are quite well and aware that their father has passed but believed that happened long ago. It was better for them to believe he had passed than the cold reality of truth. After arriving in America, our dear Vittoria met a wonderful Italian man whom she fell in love with and married. His work and family were in Chicago, Illinois, where they soon put down their roots. Francesco and I struggled in New York, and times were hard. Vittoria's husband came from a very powerful family who extended their hand to help us, but as you probably know, Francesco was as stubborn as he was kind, so of course, he refused. Only when our oldest daughter became very ill with influenza did he come to the realization that our lives were at stake there in New York. My daughters and I went to live with Vittoria and her wealthy family. Francesco and I made an agreement that it would be only for a short time until he could earn enough to rent a proper home for his family," the lovely woman acknowledged.

"We continued to live at a distance for nearly five years. Francesco never stopped sending all the money he could to us. Then one day, there he was, standing in Vittoria's kitchen. He was as handsome as I remembered, and my heart was so full," she continued.

The story that swept across the lips of her perfectly applied red lipstick could've been told through her eyes as easily as through her mouth, Mr. Townsley thought. The depth of their soft darkness revealed the tenderness she still held for dear Francesco. Mr. Townsley did not interrupt her tale of what seemed more like a long overdue confession.

"That day, Francesco and I discussed our situation here in America for many hours. It was his feeling that a family should remain together despite all outside influences. Francesco had retained an apartment in New Jersey and felt it would be a better place to raise our girls. I could not agree with him on that day. Our daughters had so much opportunity in Chicago that was almost impossible in New Jersey. Our daughters enjoyed the life of well-brought-up Chicago young ladies. They were involved in ballet and many other civic organizations. How could we ask them to give that up? We each had a choice to make. Such an unfair and difficult choice for so many of us immigrants. Life was unfair, jobs were unfair, and the promise of prosperity was an unfair luxury immigrants were kept at a distance from. When Francesco left that day, we agreed that I would remain in Chicago to raise our family with Vittoria's family, and he would go back to New Jersey and begin again," she said as she bowed her head.

"I can see him still," as she closed her dark eyes and spoke, "standing against the open doorway, the sounds of the street spilling in to fill the room, a hint of sparkle reflecting off his black hair, and that all too familiar look of sadness in disengaging another segment of life surrendered to the drive and necessity of an immigrant."

The driver, the strange woman, and Mr. Townsley were all silent, perhaps to show respect for another sacrifice made by dear Francesco.

"Forgive me, madam," Mr. Townsley pierced the silence first. "I'm afraid I do not understand why or how Francesco would then go on to marry Concetta?"

Her dark eyes had now returned to the present day, and the beautiful memory door was once again closed. She peered at Mr. Townsley and said, "I mean no disrespect, but when did your people come to America, sir?"

Mr. Townsley proudly replied, "My Norwegian ancestors came here in the 1600s."

"Of course," she agreed. "Their stories and sacrifices are known but to history alone. Try to imagine, if you can, for Francesco and me, it was a different time, a different place, with different requirements. As heartbreaking as it was, on that last day I met with Francesco, we had to be nonexistent to the other to survive. He needed to forge ahead and make way for tomorrow as if the other one of us had died. I did not possess his bravery and, therefore, chose to remain in a safe environment. My whole life has been governed by fear. It is only today, out of respect for dear Francesco, that I come here. Perhaps he reached down from heaven and released me from my bondage of fear that so cruelly I allowed to dictate my every step throughout life. I am glad to have met a friend of Francesco and know that he lived the life I had always known he would. We have a long journey ahead and must depart for Chicago now. I thank you for your kindness to Francesco and my prayers to him in heaven for he now has found a home where he truly is not a foreigner. Surely his kindness has gained the favor of our Lord."

With that statement, she motioned the driver forward, and Mr. Townsley was left standing in the soft grass of the cemetery path. His footprints sunken ever so slightly into the earth. He stood and stared up the path long after the car had traveled through the gate, turned right, and disappeared into the past. He thought of his dear friend and all the trials he never knew about. So much of immigrant life must've been a silent, longing pain. *Sadness in parting, sadness in struggle, and sadness in loss. This was the hidden life of an immigrant,* thought Mr. Townsley.

Twenty-Five

The journey back to the little stone house on the hill was uneventful for Mr. Townsley. Upon arrival, his eyes noticed three cars with Illinois plates in front of Concetta's home. None, however, belonged to the stranger he had encountered. He thought about asking one of those occupants about the unusual encounter with a strange woman, but what would be the purpose except to satisfy his own curious nature? There was no point to upsetting the family now. Mr. Townsley never shared the stranger's story with Concetta, Maria, or anyone. He owed that to his dear friend, Francesco.

As the sun tucked itself beneath the horizon that evening, the family that Francesco had served and provided for so well mourned their great loss. Francesco had left a legacy of family, a legacy of love, and a legacy to be American.

The years now evaporated away like the dew exposed to the morning sun. Concetta grew old in her loneliness for Francesco. Her comfort was in knowing that her dear Francesco was in heaven with his beautiful, sweet Nicolena, whom he had missed so much throughout his life. Shortly after Francesco passed away, Concetta's hair had turned the color of fresh cotton. Her once twinkling eyes had now dulled under the grinding of time. Some days she would sit for hours and speak of her younger days in Calabria. Carefree days of youth and tangerine sunsets brought sweet memories to Concetta.

Maria enjoyed those verbal memories with Concetta as they were previously not spoken of prior to her mind aging. Concetta had experienced several strokes in the later part of her life. As an apparent side effect, she spoke more openly of her precious parents and experiences during her life in Italy. Maria enjoyed her recollections partly because they gave Concetta such joy in remembering, and Maria felt a closeness and connection with the grandparents she never knew who lived and died across the sea.

Maria now took care of the household, garden, and her daughter, Mary, but Maria never married. She was loyal and kind to so many; perhaps her love was so vast it wasn't meant to be confined to only one person in a marriage but spread over countless others who thirst for kindness, like a much-needed rain in the desert, quenching the need of all.

In the wink of an eye, time had forged ahead. The 1950s was a decade everyone just sort of "found themselves in." The 1940s had been so filled with war, loss, and rebuilding lives that many people seemed to have drifted through that decade in an unwelcome fog. Mary found herself in high school and employed at the local theatre ticket booth. Citizens were again enjoying themselves, and the picture show was a great way to do that. WWII had become a memory the town had learned to live with and move forward without those precious citizens lost to war. Hearts and minds were once again opening to one another, and attitudes were changing all around the world. There had been enough suffering and persecution for this lifetime. The little town of Mineral Point welcomed immigrants, many of whom were war heroes, with open arms, and each citizen became a glistening thread in the fabric of this warm community.

The little house on the hill was once again alive and bustling with Italians daily. The absence of Francesco was palpable, but everyone slowly learned to live again, as he would've wanted. Concetta, while in failing health, remained the matriarch of the family. Respect for her was well regarded by all those who knew her, and this was apparent whenever visitors entered her home. Friends and family would sit and listen for hours as she spoke. Her memories were vivid, precise, and consuming. For those fortunate enough to listen, it was evident Concetta was not just remembering but immersing herself within the memory as if it were a current event.

On that last night, as Maria pulled the cotton sheet under Concetta's chin and kissed her forehead, Maria stepped back and lingered next to the bed. She stood there trying to consider all Concetta had been through, but it was far too overwhelming for thought.

As Maria left the room, she turned to whisper, "I love you, Mama," and out the door she went.

The hallway was small and stuffy, and the boards underfoot creaked with each step. *If only I could open that door at the end of the hall*, Maria thought. The outer door had swelled due to the summer heat and now was too big for the doorframe. The bottom of the door was wedged tight by the stone threshold. Maria gave it a tug to attempt some ventilation. She couldn't budge it, no matter how hard she pulled. She slipped into another bedroom and opened a window. A steamy breeze whispered in past Maria's right shoulder. The sensation left her with an uneasy, unidentifiable concern, but she shrugged it away as the movement of air improved the stuffiness of the hallway.

As the night progressed, Maria's sleep was elusive. It seemed as if the entire universe was unsettled that evening. Shortly before daybreak, the startling sound of Concetta's coughing awoke Maria. She sprang to her feet and bolted to her mother's room. It was from the doorway of that dark, humid hallway that Maria first realized the frailty of her beautiful mother. Overnight, Concetta had suddenly appeared ashen and weak in Maria's eyes. Maria was certain that everyone else had noticed this decline in health many months prior, but it took until this last moment for Maria's heart to believe.

Maria's footsteps were light across the wood floor leading up to the bed. As she reached her destination, she sat down lightly beside her mother, stroked her gleaming silver hair, and spoke ever so gently. Maria recalled earlier days from the memories Concetta had shared of living in Calabria. She reminded Concetta of the lemon trees and the olive groves. Maria spoke of moments from her own youth, sweet and comforting to remember. Concetta's tired face expressed a simple smile while Maria spoke.

"Should we get you ready for the day, Mama?" Maria inquired.

"Not just now," Concetta whispered through a cough, "I'm just too tired today."

There had been several times when Concetta requested to just lie in bed, and Maria would interject and insist that she rise and dress; today was different. Maria let Concetta remain in bed resting. Perhaps it was the sudden realization of frailty or the premonition of events that stepped in to allow Concetta the peace she so richly deserved. Whichever the case, Concetta remained in her room that day.

As family members arrived for their daily visits, it became evident that Concetta was gaining momentum to let go of her earthly life and return home with Francesco. Many family members and friends remained at the stone cottage to pray for Concetta. Maria never left her side and tended to her mother's every need. At one point, Concetta spoke to Francesco out loud, and Maria hoped with sincerity that he was in the room with them. After all, he had guided Concetta in almost every aspect of their lives. Of course, he would be there to usher her home.

It must've been about three o'clock in the afternoon when Concetta stopped responding to Maria. She simply lay there with her eyes closed as if asleep, resting peacefully within the life she created. How does the culmination of an entire lifetime of experience come down to a few poignant moments? There were moments in those last hours when Concetta must've been dreaming of the happy times in her life, and joy was visible on her face. No pain or suffering. She had already paid that debt throughout her life, many times over.

Each of Concetta's children sat with her throughout the afternoon and evening, speaking softly and sweetly about memories and dreams they each had achieved, acknowledging the struggles of their now fatigued mother. How much she had endured in her lifetime, how much she had given of herself in the struggle to succeed in their new homeland, and how much of her would always remain in their hearts.

Maria took her turn in expressing her love and gratitude. She took her mother's hand in hers and gazed for a time at its appearance. *When did your hands become old?* she wondered. Her skin was still the beautiful bronze color of fall sunsets, but now its thinness gave way to transparency, allowing each life-feeding vessel exposure to the eye. Her fingers had grown crooked, bent, and sore with the passage of time but still possessed the love for all others as they lay silent and still. The hands that led a family in prayer, the hands that worked tirelessly to build a family, the hands that now rest in complete accomplishment.

By eight that evening, all Concetta's children were present in the room. Suddenly, and without warning, Concetta opened her ebony eyes as if waking from a long nap. At first, she appeared a bit bewildered as she scanned the room, making eye contact with each child. She noted the familial similarities within each of their faces and the sadness each carried. She thought about her parents, dear sweet Nicolena, and Francesco. Oh, how she missed each of them. She then focused her fatigued attention on her children and began to utter a quiet phrase.

"I am Italian, but you, my children, are also American," she quietly whispered as her eyes peacefully closed and a smile swept across her aged face. It was her final statement of life's accomplishments to share with her children. Perhaps it was her way of keeping that thought at the forefront of their lives—a simple way of communicating the culmination of a lifelong struggle. The weight of her words resonated within each of her children, for they had witnessed many of the painstaking steps her journey took to reach this day.

A short time later, the group was startled by the noise of the hallway door swinging open. The same door that previously was stuck shut now swung freely on its hinge, unaffected by the swelled threshold. It was at this moment Concetta saw him. Her heart was once again warmed with his presence. It was her dear, caring Francesco coming to collect her once more. Behind him, breaking through the shadows, Concetta could begin to focus on others. First her dear daughter Nicolena smiling sweetly, then her father. Giovanni, and Maria, her mother. Concetta was so happy to see them, and they appeared overjoyed to see her. Concetta reached out to them and took Francesco's hand. Their children, seated quietly around the room, paused in sorrow at the sight of their mother's now lifeless body. The room was silent except for the swinging of the hallway door in the sultry warm breeze, the sniffles of anguish from Concetta's children, and the elusive miracle known only to Concetta of a family restoring its next layer of existence. As Concetta took Francesco's hand and rose from the bed, her body lay back onto the mattress, much like a feather drifting downward from above. Her ebony sparkling eyes remained closed, and she exhaled loudly. Maria quietly picked up a small timeworn sheet and covered the clock on the wall. Concetta's earthly journey was finished.

It was the beginning of the next journey for Concetta. Not so very different than the many uncertain journeys she had ventured on throughout her earthly life, but the fare had been paid for this journey, the anxiety dismissed. Secured by a life of bravery, selflessness, struggle, and faith. And this time ... that was enough.

— // —

I learned a long time ago how to walk in a cemetery. Even now, well into my fifties, I stroll here in the chilly breeze, conscious of my every featherlike footstep. I wonder if the ground beneath has memory and can identify me from recollection, even with the changes in my shoe size. As I roam through the familiar granite markers of time, three marble crosses appear in view. Here they quietly stand, proud and timeless, in a straight line at the back of what's now referred to as the "old part" of the cemetery. Something to do with the invention of the vault and the sporadic usage of them, or lack of usage, in this section of the property. Could that be the true reason this half of the cemetery forbade further burials, or was it that all the important people as they passed away were getting too close to the immigrant burial areas? A question with no real answer but deserves consideration. However, it now seems fitting to separate these courageous and undauntable people from the ordinary citizen.

Their placement is now poised forever in history. They have earned the right to be singled out as an indestructible force in their lives and now in perpetual rest. They truly possessed the passion, the hunger, and the drive to bring their families to more, despite struggles, despite pain, despite the cost. Even though most never lived to see the glories of their sacrifice, their stories need to be told, respected, and remembered. Their heirs have reaped the good fortunes each immigrant set out for. They've lived out their dreams, and we owe them a great debt of constant awareness. They were successful in their endeavor to become Americans, and they paved the pathway for all of us. They were successful in their quest to be accepted into the weavings of society, but only after their own life was finished. They were successful in their pursuit of happiness, even during their trials of sadness. They held an immeasurable bounty of perseverance, were an enormous vessel of reinvention of self, mastered a massive strength against diversity, and sustained a monumental capacity of courage. They did all this every moment, every day, until their last breath … and

that

was

enough.

About the Author

Peggy Glendenning was born, raised and educated in the rolling hills of southwest Wisconsin. She is a retired Registered Nurse and had the privilege of serving her neighbors in that capacity for 30 years. Peggy is the mother of four grown children, grandmother to four grandchildren, and proud maternal great granddaughter to Concetta and Francesco Nardi, the main characters in *That Was Enough*.

Since hanging up her stethoscope, Peggy has traveled much of Europe where she trod the footsteps of her ancestors in both Italy and Ireland. The endless tales and heroics of immigrant travels have not only enchanted her but instilled a sense of responsibility to share what is known of their personal experiences before their story is lost to history.

One of Peggy's proud accomplishments was making a pilgrimage to the small Italian village of Simbario, accompanied by her mother and two youngest sons. To return to the point of origin of their Italian heritage with three generations was a pivotal moment in Peggy's life. Walking the streets of Simbario, entering San Rocco church, gave Peggy the inspiration to write the incredible story of Francesco and Concetta.

Peggy currently resides in Iowa with her husband of 42 years where together they enjoy reading, travel, spending time with beloved family, and living out the dream set forth by their brave immigrants.

Printed in the United States
by Baker & Taylor Publisher Services